## "I thought I'd never see you again," Liza whispered

"Five years, Duke. Five years of wondering."

Something in her voice must have touched him, as his cool expression gave way to sudden pain. "Whatever I shared with you, it must have been spectacular," he answered.

Liza stepped closer, all thoughts of safety or caution evaporating, pushed aside by her feelings for the man who stood before her. She didn't wait for him to kiss her. She stood on tiptoe and brushed her lips softly against his. "I've dreamed of this moment for five years," she said, her arms going around his neck.

For a moment, Duke merely accepted her kiss, but then his arms closed around her and Liza gave herself to the pleasure of his mouth on hers.

The soft darkness of the night cloaked them, and Liza felt Duke's hands grasp her waist. Her heart was pounding, and beneath his shirt she could feel his answering heartbeat.

He eased her away from him and looked into her eyes. His own were glazed with desire.

"Liza," he said, his voice hoarse, "I remember."

Dear Harlequin Intrigue Reader,

Your summer reading list just wouldn't be complete without the special brand of romantic suspense you can only get from Harlequin Intrigue.

This month, Joanna Wayne launches her first-ever miniseries! You loved the Randolph family when you met them in her book *Family Ties* (#444). So now they're back in RANDOLPH FAMILY TIES, beginning with Branson's story in *The Second Son* (#569). Flesh and blood bind these brothers to each other—and to a mystery baby girl. All are her protectors...one is her father.

Familiar, the crime-solving black cat, is back in his *thirteenth* FEAR FAMILIAR title by Caroline Burnes. This time he explores New Orleans in *Familiar Obsession* (#570).

It had been Hope Fancy's dream to marry Quinn McClure, but not under a blaze of bullets! Are *Urgent Vows* (#571) enough to save two small children...and a lifelong love? Find out with Harlequin Intrigue author Joyce Sullivan.

With her signature style and Native American characters and culture, Aimée Thurlo revisits the Black Raven brothers from *Christmas Witness* (#544). In *Black Raven's Pride* (#572), Nick Black Raven would die to protect Eden Maes, the one-time and always love of his life. And he'd be damned before anyone would touch a hair on the head of *their* child.

So if you can handle the heat, pull the trigger on all four Harlequin Intrigue titles!

Sincerely,

Denise O'Sullivan
Associate Senior Editor
Harlequin Intrigue

# Familiar Obsession
## Caroline Burnes

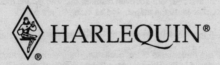

HARLEQUIN®

TORONTO • NEW YORK • LONDON
AMSTERDAM • PARIS • SYDNEY • HAMBURG
STOCKHOLM • ATHENS • TOKYO • MILAN • MADRID
PRAGUE • WARSAW • BUDAPEST • AUCKLAND

ISBN 0-373-22570-9

FAMILIAR OBSESSION

## ABOUT THE AUTHOR

Caroline Burnes continues her life as doorman and can opener for her six cats and three dogs. E. A. Poe, the prototype cat for Familiar, rules as king of the ranch, followed by his lieutenants, Miss Vesta, Gumbo, Chester, Maggie the Cat and Ash. The dogs, though a more lowly life form, are tolerated as foot soldiers by the cats. They are Sweetie Pie, Maybelline and Corky.

## Books by Caroline Burnes

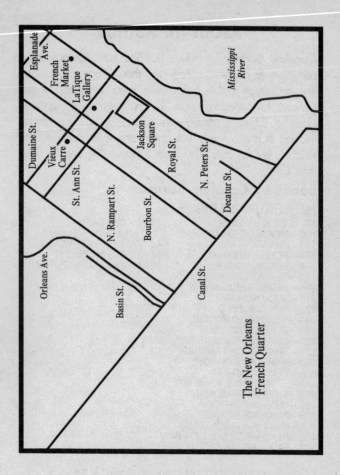

The New Orleans
French Quarter

# CAST OF CHARACTERS

*Familiar*—The feline detective is always ready to help a beautiful woman in distress.

*Liza Hawkins*—She thought the world ended when her lover disappeared. Now she's seeing his face everywhere and fears she's going crazy.

*Mike Davis, aka Duke Masonne*—He's come back to reclaim his past and the woman who once loved him.

*Anita Blevins*—Art critic and general pain, she seems to play both sides of the fence.

*Lisbeth Dendrich*—Marcelle's best friend drinks herself into oblivion. Is she guilty of something?

*Pascal Krantz*—Liza's agent made her a star. Does his need to control her hide something more sinister?

*Kyle LaRue*—Duke's former business partner made a tidy profit when Duke disappeared.

*Trent Maxwell*—The detective pursues Duke relentlessly. Does he believe Duke is a murderer, or is he part of the setup?

*Marcelle Ricco*—The socialite led a secret life, and died the day Duke disappeared.

For Sharon Paul, who took in a stray kitty, Simon,
and a stray author, me, and treated us
as if we were her own.

# Chapter One

*Ritzy! That's the only word to describe this event. Pass the salmon popovers lightly drizzled with dill sauce—save a bonbon with crème de cacao center. This is a party with style and substance. Even if it weren't for the food, the artwork is excellent. Especially this lovely watercolor of Dumaine Street after a spring rain. See the magnificent little calico kitty sitting on the third-floor balcony. She looks exactly like my Clotilde did when she was a sprite of a kitten.*

*It must be my advancing age, but this New Orleans artist, Liza Hawkins, looks like a child. But judging by her beautiful paintings, she's a grown-up. There's a certain sensuality in the watercolors, and a bit of sadness. Very interesting. As is the woman herself. Those long curls remind me of the tale of Rapunzel, and her long legs remind me of a runway model. The way she pays such close attention to everyone tells me that she's not the typical egomaniac artiste. Those big brown eyes look as if she's—haunted. Sad and haunted. I'll have to keep a close eye on Miss Liza Hawkins. This is her night to shine and I get the feeling she's about to burst into tears. As a cat who smells a mystery, my whiskers are a-twitchin'.*

LIZA HAWKINS WAS ALMOST afraid to glance around the crowded reception room of LaTique Gallery. The drone of conversation bouncing off the historic old brick walls was almost more than she could bear—not the noise, but the fact that so many people had come to the opening of her show. The success of the event was so stupendous that she was terrified it was all a dream. Any moment, she'd awaken to discover she was in her bed on the third floor of the gallery.

Alone.

As she had been for the past five years.

"Liza, darling, the show is superb."

She turned to speak to Anita Blevins, the art critic for the local newspaper, *The Times Picayune*. "Thanks, Anita. I'm in shock."

"You're on your way to the top," Anita predicted. "I've decided to use a photo of this opening on the section front. I know this isn't a good time for in-depth questions, so let's have lunch tomorrow for an interview."

"Sure." Liza felt as if her fairy godmother had waved a magic wand. She was thirty-five and had been painting for twenty years. No one had ever predicted success for her—except Duke.

Even the thought of him was painful. She tried to control the frown, but it was too late. She'd been caught in a moment of pain—and her manager was bearing down on her.

"Liza dear, wipe that sour expression off your face and *mingle*." Pascal Krantz's face was a mask of pleasure, but his voice was iron. "I've busted my chops to get your show this much coverage. Your pleasant lifestyle is due to the fact that your work is now selling for big bucks. Look, the television cameras are on us. *Smile!*"

Liza obediently smiled up at her manager. "Thanks, Pascal. I do appreciate it. It's way beyond all expectations. Look at the people. How did you get Delta Burke and Gerald McRaney to come?"

"They live right around the corner. Everyone likes to support a talented artist, Liza. I just had to make sure they realized how talented you are." His hand squeezed her arm. "And you are talented. The problem is that you don't believe it."

Liza nodded. She hated to talk about herself. "Thank you for arranging this. And the way the pictures are displayed is beautiful."

"You have your friend Eleanor Curry to thank for that. She recommended the artistic director for the show. And here the Currys are." He stepped back as Eleanor and Peter walked up.

"At last," Eleanor said, giving Liza a hug. "The paintings are incredible, Liza. Simply beautiful. I knew from the first time I saw your drawings in college that you were destined for great things. And now I can tell everyone you were my college roommate."

"It's a dream come true," Liza said. She was staring at her longtime friend but shifted her focus to Eleanor's handsome husband, Peter Curry. "I understand the black cat came with you." She pointed to Familiar, who was on a chair perusing the buffet table.

"He heard there was good food," Peter said. "We tried to leave him behind, but—"

"The television cameras love him!" Pascal said. "I couldn't have thought of a better ruse myself. Let him be. He's welcome to all the food he can eat. And the way he wanders around viewing the paintings. It's almost as if he were capable of judging art.''

"I wouldn't want to try to stop him from eating," Eleanor said with a laugh.

"He's the cat who was responsible for bringing you and Peter together, isn't he?" Liza asked. Her old roommate had been far luckier in love than she had. Eleanor and Peter's marriage had resulted in a beautiful daughter, Jordan, and a strong family unit. And Liza hadn't been told, but it seemed to her that Eleanor had a very telling glow. They'd have plenty to talk about when the gallery opening was over and they could have some privacy.

"Yes, Familiar was the instigator of our relationship," Eleanor said dryly. "He's, shall we say, unusual."

"Bring him with you Friday. We're scheduled for lunch, aren't—" Liza's gaze was drawn by sudden movement outside the gallery windows. LaTique was located on St. Ann Street in the French Quarter, not exactly the most lively part of town. Though the raucous Bourbon and Royal streets were only a few blocks away, St. Ann was basically residential. The building she occupied was three stories, a narrow structure with her gallery on the first floor, her studio on the second, and her apartment on the third.

"Yes, Friday at Napoleon's," Eleanor confirmed. "I want to hear all about your career, the future, the museums and galleries where your paintings are now hanging. You've come into the homestretch of success, Liza, and it's about time."

"Yes." She heard her friend's kind words and immediately sought a change of subject. Her success was phenomenal—and troubling. Instead of the total satisfaction she once expected upon achieving success, she'd found emptiness.

At one time, she'd been driven to paint the street scenes of New Orleans that had recently made her the darling of art patrons. Now, though, the watercolors were less important. Her artistic passions were something else, something darker. Something that she had to keep a secret even from her oldest friend, Eleanor Curry, who'd come all the way from Washington, D.C., for her opening.

A dark flicker of a moving shadow outside the front window of the gallery caught her attention once again. Her heart rate tripled, and she felt the flush of blood to her skin.

"Liza darling, your friend was saying that she wanted to purchase the painting of the young girl in the rain puddle."

Liza felt Pascal's strong fingers pressing into the muscles of her arm. She knew she was drifting away, fading from reality and entering her own private hell, but she couldn't stop herself.

The flicker of movement came at the edge of the window again. Her attention sharpened even as she tried to combat it with rational thought. It was only her imagination. This gallery opening, this event, was something she'd planned long ago. Five years ago. With Duke Masonne. But how the plan had changed. Now she was alone, and though the success was all hers, it was a lonely price to pay.

"Liza, are you okay?" Eleanor's brown eyes were narrowed with concern.

"Yes, of course." Liza tried to focus on the party. But again someone standing out in the shadows moved. The glint of a white face flashed in the light spilling from the big gallery windows facing the street.

Liza's heartbeat grew painful. It was insane. Duke had been gone five years, but there was something about the shadowy face that reminded her of him— made her hope it might be.

She felt her palms begin to tingle and the unpleasant sensation of perspiration on her brow.

"Liza?" Eleanor's voice came from a long way away.

"I—" What could she say? *Don't pay any attention to me. I saw my ex-lover who disappeared five years ago. I've been seeing him around town lately, standing in dark alleys, outside Grizaldi's when I go for groceries. I'm beginning to catch glimpses of him through the hanging bundles of elephant garlic and peppers at the French Market.*

"Get a chair."

She heard Pascal's order and felt her body being pushed into a chair. But her attention remained on the window. The lighting outside was poor. It could have been a figment of her imagination. Or her mind slipping toward madness. At that thought, her heart rate increased even more. She felt the room spinning.

"Ice. Bring some ice and a cloth," she heard Eleanor say.

But she couldn't answer her, couldn't reassure her that she was okay, just a little woozy and terrified.

"Don't do this now," Pascal whispered in her ear. "We can't allow this show to fall into a dramatic tragedy. Your work will be overshadowed by the drama of your behavior, Liza. Pull yourself together and stop whatever this is."

Pascal's words almost penetrated. She could feel her

heart slowing, feel her lungs expanding as she was finally able to draw in a deep breath.

And then she looked out the window.

The light from the gallery spilled clearly across the features of Duke Masonne's face. The hair was longer, the face leaner, more lined. But it was Duke.

She pushed Pascal back with a movement so abrupt she almost made him fall. In an instant, she was on her feet, the elegant black heels she'd purchased just for this event clacking on the Italian-tile floor. In five long strides, she was pulling open the door, the bell jangling madly as she dashed out into the street.

"Duke!" she called out. "Duke!"

Far at the end of the block, a young couple turned and stared at her. Other than that, the street was empty.

She felt a presence at her feet and looked down to find the cat standing beside her. "He was here," she said aloud. "I don't care what they say, I saw him. I'm not losing my mind. I'm not."

A spring breeze teased the skirt of her black dress, and Liza found that she simply couldn't return to the party. She stood on the street, the empty street, and forced her lungs to draw air in and out. She'd made a fool of herself. This was the one night when her behavior was critical, and she'd run out of her own gallery, her own party, as if she were a madwoman. The terrifying thing was that she was beginning to believe she might be completely insane. Her manager hadn't said as much, but Pascal had been worried enough about her lately to begin recommending a visit to a psychiatrist.

"Liza?"

Eleanor's soft voice and her gentle hand drew Liza back from her dark thoughts.

"Come back inside with me," Eleanor prompted.

"I can't," Lisa whispered. "I'm such a fool."

Eleanor gave her hand a comforting pat. "A fool is a long way from what you are. Now come inside. Everyone's worried about you. The best thing is to walk back in, give a smile, and then I'll say you have a migraine. I'll see that you can escape upstairs."

Liza's relief was so deep and quick that even she had to laugh weakly at her pathetic response. "Promise? I just can't stay there any longer."

"Migraine is the perfect excuse." Eleanor hesitated. "Just as long as you and I both agree that we have to get to the bottom of the real problem here. We can lie and say you have a headache, but we have to fix whatever is really wrong."

Liza started to reply, but her voice broke. She finally turned and looked into her friend's troubled brown eyes. "God, Eleanor, I don't know if I can fix it. What if I'm going insane?"

"I doubt that," Eleanor said stoutly. "I've known you for a very long time, Liza. You were never in doubt of who you were or where you wanted to go in life. I think maybe that success has caught you unprepared. It is terrifying to suddenly discover that your dreams have come true. Lots of people have trouble adjusting. That's what you're going through—a scary adjustment period."

Liza clung to the possibility. "Do you really believe that?"

Eleanor put her arm around Liza's shoulders. "I do. But first things first. Let's go back inside, smile and show everyone that you're fine. Then we'll escape. Okay?"

"Okay." With Eleanor's support and the black cat

at her heels, Liza steeled herself against the trauma of reentering the gallery. She met the expectant faces of her guests with a smile.

"I'm so sorry," she said. "My head." She reached up to touch her temple, aware of the black humor associated with such a gesture. To children, such a gesture meant someone was "touched in the head."

"It's a migraine," Eleanor said. "Liza used to have them in college. Blinding pain, you know. The terrible, terrible stress of being so talented and being the center of attention." She said the last lightly.

"Yes, sudden success can be traumatizing," Pascal Krantz added as he came to Liza's other side. "I should have expected this. Liza is so shy and retiring. All of this attention, why it's just too much!"

"Yes," Liza agreed. She gave Pascal's arm a squeeze. He'd picked up perfectly on Eleanor's cue, and she could see clearly that soon she'd be able to escape the party, to retire to the privacy of her third-floor apartment. Pascal and Eleanor would make it okay.

"Liza's sensitive to light," Eleanor said. "I'm going to put her to bed in a dark room and call the doctor."

Before anyone could say anything further, Eleanor led Liza to the small elevator at the back of the gallery.

"A million thanks," Liza whispered.

"Thank me by getting to the bottom of this," Eleanor answered.

*THE ELEVATOR DOOR is about to shut, but a fast black cat can make it. Whew! Thank goodness I dropped that extra pound I gained at Christmas. Another sixteen ounces and I would have been a crushed kitty.*

*So I'm headed up to the artist's lair. How exciting. And even better, the color is returning to Liza's face. For a minute there, I thought she might actually have seen a ghost.*

*What did she see? By the time I got to the street, it was empty. But she saw something. Or she thought she did.*

*Now as a student of humanoids, I'd say that Liza thought she saw something terrible. She had the look of a person who's witnessed a tragic accident. A wreck. A fire. A kidnapping. Something truly awful.*

*Yet she ran toward it. Which tells me that her expression and her actions are at odds. There's a medical expression for such behavior—conflicted. The only analogy I can come up with is a cat who sees a dish of grilled grouper, wants to eat it, then spits at it and runs away. In other words, a very sick kitty. Then again, artists are known for their erratic behavior.*

*I shall withhold judgment until further investigation, which I'm about to conduct right now. While Eleanor puts our little painter to bed, I'm going to inspect her digs.*

MIKE DAVIS RAN HIS FINGERS through his hair. He needed a haircut in the worst kind of way. And he missed his cowboy hat. At the thought, he felt an odd homesickness. Funny, when he'd first taken the job at Gabe and Rachel Welch's ranch, the Circle C, he'd never anticipated that he'd come to call the ten-thousand-acre spread home.

It was a home of harsh realities, in weather and in the heart. For the past five years, he'd worked every fence line, herded the cattle, birthed the calves and trained the horses. It had become home.

And now he was over a thousand miles away, in the spring humidity of New Orleans, Louisiana, wandering the streets like a...what? A ghost? A man without a home or identity?

Mike glanced in the mirror. He'd grown accustomed to seeing the reflection of his features, though truthfully, for the past five years, he'd hardly had time to stop and look at himself. Looks didn't matter much on a cattle ranch. Not for a man, a cow or a horse. It was a life where skill and talent counted for everything. Good looks—and Mike had been told by more than a few cowgirls that he had some nice features—were just an extra blessing.

But he might as well have been the phantom of the opera or the hunchback of Notre Dame, based on Liza Hawkins's reaction to him. He terrified her. And if it wasn't because of his looks, then it had to be because of his actions.

He turned away from the mirror with a growing sense of frustration and took long strides across the room to the painting he'd just purchased. He'd saved most of his wages for the past five years—plus, he had uncanny luck at poker—he could afford to live well, for a while. Liza Hawkins's painting had been irresistible. It was a watercolor so filled with afternoon light that he felt as if he'd lived the moment. He knew exactly the shade of terra-cotta that would show through in the old brick dampened by rain and then dazzled by sunlight. He knew the crooked texture of the bricks used as roadbed and the intense green of the shrubs. He *knew* that scene. But how did he know it?

More importantly, how did he know the artist, Liza Hawkins?

From the pocket of his jeans he drew out the worn business card. *Liza Hawkins, artist. 225 St. Ann. New Orleans, Louisiana.* It was the only personal possession that had been on him when he woke up in a North Dakota hospital five years before. He'd been found, beaten into unconsciousness, in a boxcar at a small train depot. Three days later, he'd regained consciousness in the intensive care unit of Dola County Hospital. From there, fate had taken hold of him with a benevolent hand.

He replaced the card and continued to examine the painting, moving slowly around his rented apartment until he'd visited all five of the canvases he'd purchased in the past five months. All were Liza's, and all depicted French Quarter scenes that somehow seemed to Mike to be a part of his personal history.

That was why he was in New Orleans—to find his past. He wasn't certain he was in the right city or the right state, but it was the only place he knew to start.

The sharp ring of the telephone drew him out of his thoughts. When he answered, he felt his face melt into a smile.

"Rachel," he said, instantly picturing the elderly woman who'd seen him in the hospital and somehow found it in her heart to want to help. "I'm fine," he reassured her. "Perfectly fine."

"Bristo's been standing in the corral looking out toward the range," Rachel Welch said. "He's pining for you, Mike. We're missing you, too. It's calving season and we're feeling the pinch."

Mike's smile increased. Rachel Welch was using both barrels to make him feel bad—his horse *and* the fact that all hands were needed during calving season on the ranch he might one day inherit.

"You know I'd be there if I could. I have to finish this. I want to be certain I'm the man you and Gabe think I am—the man you treat as your son."

There was a pause. "You *think* you have to finish it," Rachel said slowly. "Mike, whatever you were in the past, you are a son to me and Gabe now. Whatever you did, it doesn't matter to us. I've never known a better judge of a man than Gabe Welch. You've won his respect, Mike. And his heart. That's what matters, not a past that you can't even remember."

"It matters to me," Mike said slowly. "I don't even know my real name."

"Mike Davis has worked here for five years. It's a good enough name."

"Rachel, I tried to move on. You know I did. But I can't go forward until I know my past."

"I told Gabe he shouldn't have put you on the spot about the ranch. I told him just to make out the will and leave it all to you without telling you. None of this would have come up."

Mike hesitated. There was a certain amount of truth in Rachel's accusation. He'd settled into ranching, acquiring the skills and the tremendous knowledge it took to keep cattle alive and thriving through the cold North Dakota winters. Figuring ways to stretch grasslands and outwit droughts. In the long days of hard work, he'd found satisfaction and managed to keep concerns about his past at bay. But when Gabe had pulled him aside and told him that he was heir to the Circle C, Mike had found himself up against the wall of his unknown past. He couldn't allow Gabe and Rachel to hand everything they held precious and dear over to him until he was certain his past wouldn't impact his future.

"The ranch is part of it. But eventually, I would have had to learn the truth."

"Cowpatty!"

"Rachel," Mike admonished gently.

"Listen to me, Mike. The past can be like quicksand. It can pull you down into darkness. You and I both know there's a reason you don't remember. Whatever it is, you left it way behind. You have a good life up here. I'm afraid if you keep digging and digging, you're going to find something that—"

"I have to know the truth." Mike's grip on the phone increased. "Don't you see? If I can't face the truth, I'll always see myself as a coward, as a man who couldn't face up to the consequences of his past."

"Have you talked to the artist woman?"

"Not yet," Mike admitted. Even the mention of Liza Hawkins made his stomach tighten.

"Well, get on with it. Just go up to her and ask her point-blank."

Mike nodded, then realized Rachel couldn't see the gesture. "I will. It's just that whenever she catches a glimpse of me, she acts terrified. I went by her gallery tonight, and she was having a big party there. I was looking in the window and she saw me. Rachel, it was like she hated me." He didn't have to ask the question that tormented him. What if he'd hurt her in some way?

"If you're going to confront the past, then do it and get back up here. I know you'll run out of money eventually. You'll come home to us."

"I will," Mike promised. "I certainly will."

"Be careful, Mike," Rachel added. "Already I hear

a change in your voice. It's my biggest fear that you'll end up caught in the web of the past. Leave the darkness behind you, son. Come on home and work on the new life you have with me and Gabe.''

## Chapter Two

At Eleanor's direction, Liza leaned back against the sofa and accepted the cup of steaming hot tea. "Do you think I ruined the party?" she couldn't help but ask.

"'Ruin' is too strong a word. Let's say that we didn't answer all the questions, and judging from the look on Ms. Blevins's face, she doesn't intend to let what happened tonight drop." Eleanor took a seat beside the sofa. "And I have a few of my own to ask. What's going on, Liza? You were never a person given to drama and scenes."

Liza wrapped her hands around the cup and stalled for time to think through her answer. During the past five years, she'd become more and more isolated from everyone who cared about her. Painting had become her life, her only outlet. Her life had spun out of balance, leaving only her work and her desperate longing for the man who'd disappeared five years before.

She wasn't close to anyone, not even her parents. In those few years, she'd managed to alienate her artist friends in New Orleans. The blame lay on her, she knew. No matter how she'd tried to shake off Duke's disappearance, it had consumed her life. There wasn't enough left to maintain friendships. Eleanor was the only person left who'd known her for any length of time. Liza knew if she decided to come clean, Eleanor was the person she had to trust.

"Remember Duke Masonne?"

Eleanor sat up a little taller. "How could I forget him, Liza? You were in love with him. You were going to marry him. And then he disappeared." Eleanor's voice was sharp.

"Yes." Liza saw the anger in her friend's eyes. Whenever she broached the subject of Duke Masonne, her friends had one of two reactions—they hated him because they felt he'd dumped her and skipped town or they pitied her because they thought he was dead, the victim of foul play. Eleanor obviously preferred the first theory.

"That was five years ago, Liza. The cops closed the case on his disappearance. As far as everyone is concerned, he's dead." Eleanor waved her hand around. "You've moved on since then. You've become a celebrated artist with enough money to open your own gallery."

Liza sat up. "You never thought he was dead, did you?"

"My thoughts don't matter. He's dead to you. Five years, Liza. Even if he is alive somewhere, there's no excuse for a man who abandoned the woman who loved him and never had the decency to tell her goodbye or let her know that he was safe—"

"I saw him tonight." Liza saw Eleanor's reaction, though her friend attempted to mask her shock.

"Really, Liza," Eleanor said, rising to her feet. She bent over and felt Liza's forehead. "You don't feel feverish."

"I saw him outside the window. That's why I jumped up and ran out."

Eleanor looked as if she'd been slapped. "You saw Duke Masonne?"

"I've been seeing him for the past few weeks."

"Seeing him?"

Liza met her friend's gaze. "Catching glimpses of him. He's been hanging around the gallery. Sometimes when I go to buy groceries, he follows me. He's here, in New Orleans. And he's alive."

Liza pulled the comforter up around her, suddenly feeling cold, though the night was warm. A gentle breeze ruffled the curtains in the room, sending them swirling like dancing wraiths. The idea was as chilling as the expression on Eleanor's face.

"I'm not losing my mind," Liza said, forcing herself to sound more confident of that fact than she felt. "I really saw him."

"And he's stalking you." Eleanor let the words hang. At last, she leaned forward and grasped Liza's shoulders. "Listen to yourself. Can you hear what you're saying? Duke would never come back to New Orleans, not after the way he deserted you. He left you fearing for his safety, wondering if he was injured or dead. There's no coming back from an action that cruel and despicable."

Liza closed her eyes briefly. This was the reaction she'd expected, but not the one she'd hoped for. Just this once she needed an ally, someone to help her. She wasn't imagining things. Duke Masonne had been standing outside the window of LaTique Gallery. He'd been there not an hour ago, and two days before that. And a week before that. It was almost as if he wanted to come inside but couldn't bring himself to try.

"I need help," Liza said softly. She opened her eyes. "Will you help me?"

Eleanor's hands slowly slid from her friend's arms. "What can I do?"

"He's here and he's alive. I have to know what he wants."

"If that's the case, think it through. He left you wondering for five years. Yes, your career has sky-rocketed. Yes, your talent has grown. Yes, you're about to become an international success. But have you had a date in five years? Have you established any relationship with a good man? Have you had an ounce of fun in all this time?" Eleanor held up a hand. "The answer is no. A big no. Because that man left you in emotional limbo, a hell of doubt and worry and pain. *If* he is here—and that's a big if—the only thing you should give him is a kick in the pants."

Liza took a deep breath. "Everything you say is true. I am moving forward, though. I have been seeing someone. It isn't serious. Not yet, but it could grow. Maybe."

"Who?"

"Trent Maxwell. He's a New Orleans policeman. But I have to know what happened to Duke. Maybe if I find out the truth, I can put this behind me. Eleanor, you didn't really know Duke. He wasn't the kind of man who would deliberately hurt me. I...I don't know how to make you see it, but you have to believe me. What we had was very much like the love you and Peter share. It *was* real. If I can't believe that, how can I ever believe in anyone again?"

Eleanor stood up and began to pace the room. "What do you want me to do?"

"Help me find him."

"And then?"

"I only want to talk to him."

"I don't know." Eleanor came back around the sofa to face her. "I'll talk it over with Peter. But I want a promise from you."

"Anything." Liza felt a surge of hope that was the most promising emotion she'd allowed herself in five years. "What?"

"You'll go and talk with a professional, a psychologist."

Liza's immediate reaction was to reject the idea. She wasn't insane. She hadn't imagined the man outside the window. But she saw the iron in Eleanor's eyes. "I don't think this is necessary, but I'll agree. If you help me."

Eleanor nodded. "I have to go back to Washington. We left Jordan with Peter's folks, and I'm due for a doctor's appointment."

"You're pregnant, aren't you?" Liza asked.

"Yes, I think I am." Eleanor's hand strayed to her stomach and her smile was small but joyous. "I have to go back to D.C. In the meantime, though, I'll leave Familiar here with you. He's rather extraordinary. And to be honest, if Duke Masonne or his look-alike is snooping around here, Familiar will deal with him. When I return, we'll settle this once and for all."

"You're leaving the cat?" Liza looked at the black cat that was scampering around the room.

"Don't ever underestimate him," Eleanor said. "He's the best detective working the business."

"And people think I'm suffering from delusions," Liza said softly. She was rewarded by a smile from her old friend.

"Point taken," Eleanor said. "Now Pascal gave me

this sleeping pill for you. He said it would only relax you, and I want you to take it.''

Liza made a face. ''He has more pills than a pharmacist.'' She obediently opened her mouth and took the pill and glass of water Eleanor offered.

''I'm going back downstairs to help with the party. Just relax and try to rest. I'll take care of everything.''

Liza caught her friend's hand. ''Thank you, Eleanor. I've been alone for so long, I'd forgotten what it feels like to have a real friend.''

''I only hope I'm doing the right thing.''

*I HAD A WONDERFUL little snoop around Liza's establishment. Very neat. First floor, gallery, second floor, studio, and at the tip-top, her home, complete with a second, secret studio. I am gravely concerned.*

*To all the world, Liza is a watercolor artist, a woman who captures the spirit and soul of New Orleans in the wash of color, the fragility of beauty that comes from age and light and the fine details of a scene. But there is another Liza, another side to this complicated woman. A very dark side.*

*She has secret drawings in her secret studio, all pen and ink, all of one man. I have no doubt that this is the missing Duke Masonne. He may have been gone for five years, but he's been very much a part of Liza's life. There must be over a hundred drawings of him.*

*The only good thing I can say is that I have no doubt of what he looks like. Though many of the drawings are shadowy, a strange portrayal of his face half in light and half in dark, I could spot him in a lineup in a split second.*

*He is, indeed, a handsome man. Striking, even. But what truly stirs the fear in my heart is the way Liza*

*has created a shrine to him. I mean, her little secret
room is so full of him that it seems there's no room
for anything else. And I know enough about humanoid
psychology to realize that such an obsession is a long,
long way from healthy.*

*I was on the street with Liza and what I saw was
emptiness. There was no one around. Not even the hint
of someone. Not even a lingering trace of an odor.*

*Eleanor has generously offered my help in this case,
but for the first time in my career as a supersleuth, I
don't know if I'm the cat for the job. I realize I'm
smart, capable, highly trained and incredibly intuitive,
but Liza may need the help of a doctor, not a detective.
The only thing I can do is keep my sharp eyes open
and my sensitive ears attuned to the sound of a visitor.
If this Duke guy is out there, I'll nail him. And he can
answer a few questions that have waited far too long
to be addressed.*

*The only positive thing I found was a half-finished
picture—not watercolor or pen and ink but acrylic—
so very different from anything else she's done.
There's a sense of fantasy to it—a robbery in progress
depicted from the point of view of a bystander. And
the loot being stolen is a painting. Bright colors, a
sense of whimsy. If this is the new direction her work
is taking, perhaps she's going to leave her dark memories behind. Then again, if she's seeing this Duke
Masonne in every shadow and behind every bush, it
doesn't seem to me as if she's ready to step out of the
past.*

*Ah, her sleeping pill is taking effect. She's one beau-
tiful woman, and so childlike with that long blond hair
falling over the sofa and onto the floor.*

*If this Duke is alive, why would he abandon a*

*woman like this? That's the question I somehow have
to make her consider. Was he a criminal with a secret
life? Did he get into some kind of trouble? Was he
killed? Five years and no one has an answer. Now
that seems more than a little strange to me. I suppose
there's just so dang many humanoids running around
the planet that it's impossible to keep up with every
single one.*

*Now I'm going to do a little more snooping while
Miss Renoir sleeps.*

THE AFTERNOON HAD GROWN warm, and Mike slipped
out of his jacket and carried it over his arm. The
French Quarter was bustling during what he'd come
to view as a typical Friday morning as tourists made
one more attempt to seek out the delicious food and
the flavor of the old Quarter.

He'd had a restless night, endlessly going over Liza
Hawkins's expression when she'd seen him in the window. The predominant emotion had been fear. But beneath that, there was something else. Something that
made his own body respond in a way he'd long forgotten.

She was a beautiful woman, and desire for her
would not have been unusual. There was more to it,
however. Desire and something electric. They had a
past, of that he was certain. What kind of past, though?
That was the question.

He was tempted to stroll by her gallery again, but
thought better of it. He'd frightened her badly.
Chances were she had someone on the lookout for
him.

For several weeks he'd confined his activities to
shadowing her. He knew her daily habits, the place

she bought her groceries, the restaurants she frequented, dining mostly alone. Except for the tall blond man. A cop. He was a plainclothes detective—Mike hadn't had any trouble finding that out. Trent Maxwell was well known in the French Quarter.

The first time he'd seen Liza with the cop, he'd felt a stab of jealousy so visceral he'd felt his hands clench into fists and his body tense for action. It had been a gut reaction and he'd been able to control it. But he hadn't been able to explain it. Not to his satisfaction.

He felt things for Liza Hawkins, but he didn't understand why. The answer was buried in the past, and today he'd decided to stop watching and start getting some answers.

He picked up a *Times Picayune* newspaper and hurried back to his apartment. The article about Liza's opening was on the front of the art section, a splashy story with several photographs that lauded Liza's talent and her "meteoric rise" to success.

Anita Blevins was the art critic whose byline headed the story, and Mike picked up the phone, dialed the paper and waited for the switchboard to connect him with the critic. Her voice was stiff, cultured and impatient, just as he'd anticipated.

"My name is Mike Davis and I just read your article on a New Orleans artist, Liza Hawkins. I'm interested in collecting some of her work, but I wondered if you might have more details about her."

"I'm not the woman's biographer," Anita Blevins said sharply.

"But as a journalist with a great degree of talent, as demonstrated in your article, I was hoping you might give me an unprejudiced opinion and a bit of history. Of course, if you're too busy, I understand."

"A bit of history?" Anita's voice warmed. "Okay, a thumbnail sketch. New Orleans artist, watercolorist, single, had a tragic love affair with a businessman, very reclusive and eccentric. Pretty standard fare for artists of all types, I'd say."

Mike wasn't the least bit interested in the value of Liza's work, but he knew that was the tack to take. "Do you believe her work will increase in value?"

"No doubt. Are you an investor or a collector?" Anita's interest was aroused.

"Both. I collect what I like, but I also like to turn a profit." Mike was almost surprised at the ease with which the words came. He didn't remember investing in anything except cattle feed and fertilizer. Or sometimes a good bull. He'd seen hefty returns on two prize Herefords.

"Buy her now. She's going straight up. And the pictures are a bonus. They are quite beautiful, aren't they?"

"I think so."

"Are you a native of New Orleans, Mr. Davis? You don't have the accent, but then our city is so culturally rich that diversity is almost a trademark."

"I'm visiting," Mike said carefully. "Why does Miss Hawkins paint only New Orleans scenes?"

"That's a good question. When I interview her, I'll ask. You can read the answer in my profile of her for the Sunday paper."

"I'll look forward to it." He could tell she was about to bolt off the telephone. "You said she was involved with a businessman. What happened?"

"He disappeared. You asked for facts, but do you want supposition?"

Mike's hand clenched at his side. "Facts are wonderful, but a report with intuition can sometimes ferret out the truth even when it can't be proven." Anita Blevins was a woman susceptible to flattery, and he used it without shame.

"There are two theories. Duke Masonne was murdered and the body will never be found or...he was involved in illegal deals on the docks and he disappeared."

"What did this Masonne do?"

"He imported art and antiques from Europe. Quite the complement to our artist. It was an odd match in some ways, a conservative businessman and an artist. That kind of difference breeds gossip. And don't think I'm going to repeat any of it. Use your imagination."

"You've been more than helpful. I'll look forward to your profile," Mike said.

"You've piqued my interest, Mr. Davis. It might be fun to do an article on an investor who collects local artists. What about it?"

"And ruin my cloak of anonymity? Not today. But if I change my mind, I'll give you a call." He hung up quickly, hoping the newspaper didn't use caller identification. He'd been foolish to call from his apartment.

"Duke Masonne." He said the name softly. At last he had a place to start.


LIZA CLOSED THE SCRAPBOOK and found herself staring into the golden gaze of Familiar. The cat had sat on the arm of her sofa as if he'd guarded her all night long. Incredible, but she did have the strangest sense that she was safe as long as he was there. Either it was that sentiment or the sleeping pill, she wasn't sure which, but she'd actually slept better the past night than she had in weeks.

Her fingers traced the leather cover of the scrapbook. "It was real," she said to the cat. "No matter what anyone tries to tell me, the love Duke and I shared was real. He didn't leave me. He didn't run off. Something happened. And now he's back here to explain."

Even to herself, she sounded pathetic—a woman jilted who can't accept the fact. If Duke was alive, then he'd left her. Five years. Why hadn't he called? Why hadn't he simply said he was leaving? She wasn't the kind of woman who clung to a man. She'd never been. If he'd asked for his freedom, she would have let him go without a scene or a recrimination. He knew that.

At least she would have been spared five years of hell. Five long years of wondering, of imagining. Of hoping.

She stood up and put the scrapbook on the coffee table. To her surprise, it was almost dusk. Not even Pascal had called to interrupt her sleep. He must be inordinately worried about her, she thought wryly. Normally no one's problems or concerns came before Pascal's. He'd been known to browbeat an artist for a commissioned picture while the artist's mother was dying of cancer.

"I should get dressed," she said. Talking to the cat was becoming a habit and one that concerned her. Not only was she seeing men who'd disappeared, she was talking to a cat as if he could understand every syllable.

"How about a stroll through the French Market? I'm starving. Maybe we can find some suitable food."

"Meow!"

"Now that's enthusiasm. Eleanor didn't think to leave cat food for you."

"Grr-rrr-rr-rr."

"Oh, so cat food is out of the question."

"Meow."

She was losing her mind. The cat was talking back to her—and she understood him perfectly. "I'll take a shower and get dressed. You consider the menu."

She rushed through her toilet and dressed. When she came back into the room wearing pale yellow capris, sandals and a cotton pullover, she found the cat on the sofa with the telephone book open. His paw was on an ad for soft-shell crabs.

"This is what you want?" She knew it was. "Okay, my fine feline detective. Soft-shells it will be. And I'll pick up some fresh fruit and vegetables for me. If we're going to solve this problem, we'll both need our strength."

Familiar scampered into the elevator with her and in a moment they were on the sidewalk. She noticed that Pascal had even hung the Closed sign on the door. He'd allowed her to violate one of his cardinal business rules—closing the gallery on a weekday was usually unthinkable, especially after an opening. At the memory of the party and her behavior, a flush touched her cheeks. She had acted as if she'd lost her mind. No matter what she'd seen, no one else had seen it. And people were always looking for a reason to think she was on the verge of a breakdown. She'd given them a fine display. At the corner she bought a newspaper and then headed toward the Café du Monde for a hot beignet and some café au lait. For Familiar she ordered a saucer of fresh cream, which she surreptitiously served under the table to the amusement of several patrons of the open-air café.

The breeze blew off the Mississippi River, which was only fifty yards away, and Liza sipped her coffee and read Anita Blevins's review of her opening. The story was wonderful, and the reporter had failed to even mention Liza's strange behavior. She had Pascal to thank for that, Liza knew. He was incredible at manipulating the media and controlling an artist's image. It was something they'd had several difficult arguments about, but she couldn't deny he was masterful at it.

She kept only the arts section of the newspaper, leaving the rest for whoever might take her table. Then she signaled to Familiar that she was ready to walk. They headed east, passing the expensive shops of Jackson Brewery with their window displays and the smells of homemade confections and spicy foods.

The French Market was the best place in New Orleans for fresh vegetables, sunglasses, silver jewelry, T-shirts and a host of other objects.

She stopped at a vegetable vendor and selected an eggplant, onions, fresh tomatoes and fresh basil, always aware that Familiar was right at her feet. He was an incredible creature, making himself at home without getting in anyone's way.

She passed an elderly woman with a display of voodoo dolls, giving the small stick-and-moss figures only a cursory glance.

"Buy one for protection," the old woman said.

"What?" Liza felt her stomach twist at the words. They'd come so unexpectedly and tapped into her deepest fears. She looked into the old woman's eyes—cloudy from cataracts.

"You're in need of protection," the old woman said softly. "The specter of the past follows you." She selected a doll dressed in red gingham. "Take this one. Keep it close to you."

"I don't need protection." Liza spoke the words without conviction. Something about the old woman unsettled her.

"Suit yourself." She replaced the doll. "I see darkness around you. Shadows that spring to life. I can make you a gris-gris to keep the bad spirits at bay."

"No. No thank you." Liza started to back away. She felt the cat at her ankles and she suddenly heard him hiss.

Liza looked back toward the vegetable vendors she'd just left. Duke Masonne was standing there, his dark gaze following every move she made.

# Chapter Three

"Liza." Mike spoke her name, but it was too soft for her to hear. He was frozen by her terrified expression. He'd followed her to the French Quarter, hoping that in the open, among the crowds, he could approach her. There was so much to talk about, so much to tell. He'd discovered his identity! And so much more. He'd learned that five years before, Liza Hawkins had been the most important thing in his life.

His first impulse had been to find her, to confide in her. To see if she held the key that would fully unlock his past. But his actions had set up a chain reaction in Liza. He had to get her to listen to him long enough to figure out why he terrified her so. He'd put her old, worn business card in the inside pocket of his shirt. If he could show it to her, make her understand that it was his only link to the past, maybe she would talk to him.

He reached inside his jacket and knew instantly that the motion had been misinterpreted. Liza's eyes widened, her gaze riveted on the movement of his hand. To his horror, she turned and fled. Bumping into tourists, stumbling over vendors and their wares, she left a trail of destruction behind her as she darted through the French Market and toward the open area of the levee. Scampering after her was a strange black cat.

"Liza!" He found his voice and called after her, but it only seemed to spur her to run faster. She'd assumed he was reaching for a weapon! He knew it, and he realized how foolish his action had been. He didn't have a choice. If he was going to talk with her, he'd have to run her down. He started after her at a wide-open sprint.

Her long hair fluttered behind her in a banner of flaxen gold, and Mike felt his heart contract. He could almost remember the feel of that hair in his hands, brushing across his face, teasing his skin as he slept beside this woman who was terrified of him. What had he done to her?

In the newspaper articles he dug up at the library, he'd found out more details about his disappearance. Five years before, he'd vanished from New Orleans, his business, and Liza's life. For several months the police had continued to search for him, but he'd vanished without a trace.

The articles were filled with speculation about his "possible murder." And the docks were thoroughly searched for his body. Which was never found.

The pieces of the past had begun to slip into place. Mike wasn't sure what had happened to him—all he really knew was that he'd been severely beaten. His nearly dead body had been found in a boxcar at a train depot in North Dakota, and he'd been taken to the hospital as a John Doe. There, Gabe and Rachel Welch had seen him and given him the name Mike Davis.

For a man who had no memory of working cattle, he took to it like a natural. His hands toughened, and the rest of his body became strong and lean, thriving on hard work. And for five long years he'd spent many an endless night wondering who and what he'd been before he woke up in North Dakota.

He slowed his sprint once he was close enough to Liza to keep her in his sights. He'd decided to trail after her until she was tired. That way, he might have a better chance to explain himself. He had an inkling of what she must be feeling—fear and fury. Unless the newspaper and local magazines had doctored their stories, he and Liza had been deeply in love. For five years she'd lived with his seeming abandonment.

She was only thirty yards ahead of him, running along the levee—running away from the bustling French Market and the tourist area. He knew she was reacting blindly, and that when she realized that she was running into a trap, she'd be only that much more afraid of him. Somehow he had to think of a way to calm her.

She was tiring and beginning to slow. And she'd begun to realize her miscalculation—he could see the panic in the quick way she turned left and right, hunting for a way back. He knew that in the last fading light of the day, he blocked her path.

"Liza," he called out. "Liza, I only want to talk to you."

She finally stopped. With what had to be great courage, she swung around to face him, half her face and body silhouetted against the beauty of the spring sunset. She stood on the levee, the west side still awash in the dying light and the east side, where land met river, only a black shadow.

"Who are you?" she called back. "What do you want?"

"I only want to talk." She was so incredibly beau-

tiful that it almost took his breath away. Her fear was
his pain. "I don't have a weapon." He held open both
sides of his coat to show his chest. "I don't want to
hurt you. I just want to talk."

"Leave me alone." Her voice broke and he could
hear the tears in her voice. "Please, please, just leave
me alone. I'm begging you. Quit scaring me.
Please…"

Something in her voice struck a familiar chord and
he hesitated. He'd loved her once with all his heart.
He knew it. He could feel the memory of it. And he
was terrifying her. It was wrong. He had to back off
and give her a chance to talk to him willingly. He
couldn't just herd her down the levee and corral her
as he would a stray cow.

"Liza, I'm going—"

The gunshot rang out and Mike felt the bullet whiz
only a millimeter from his head. He ducked instinctively and rolled down the side of the levee toward
the black current of the river. It was a steep incline,
and he lost control, his body tumbling against the hard
rocks that marked the edge of the Mississippi River.

Liza's scream was a piercing wail of horror and
fear.

"Stop!" she cried out. "Stop!"

Another shot blasted the night and fragments of
rock exploded only a few inches from Mike's leg. He
forced his body to remain perfectly still. He was hidden in the darkness. As long as he didn't panic, he
was safe. Or relatively so. He listened intently, hoping
for that telltale noise that would alert him to his at-
tacker's whereabouts.

Working on the ranch, Mike had often faced the
dangers of nature. To his knowledge, he'd never been

attacked by another human being—except that he'd once been almost beaten to death and nearly died in a boxcar. Not exactly something a mountain lion or grizzly would do. The problem was, he didn't remember any of that. He didn't remember why someone had wanted to kill him.

But someone did. Someone remembered very well and seemed to have come to finish the job.

Mike wasn't certain he could swim, but he couldn't just hunker down and wait for someone to kill him. He slipped into the water and was startled by its depth. With the darkness for cover, his best chance to escape injury or possible death was to swim back downriver. As he let the swift current of the big river take him, he discovered that he could, at least, swim.

LIZA RECOGNIZED Trent Maxwell after the first shot. She'd been relieved to see him until the second shot. It registered on her then that he was firing on a man who was possibly already injured and might be unarmed.

She rushed toward Trent and grabbed his arm, pulling the gun down. "Trent, stop it. Have you lost your mind?" She stared into the darkness where she could only hear the river lapping hungrily at the rocks. "My God, did you kill him?" Her emotions were ricocheting in all directions. She'd been terrified of the man who was chasing her, but she also felt a rushing need to protect him.

"I missed him. Are you okay?" Trent grasped both of her shoulders though he kept his grip on the gun and a wary eye on the side of the levee. "Who was that man? What did he want?"

Liza found that she couldn't answer. She shook her

head and was comforted by Trent's strong hands as he rubbed her arms. She was suddenly extremely cold. Despite the warm spring night, she shivered violently.

"Hey, it's okay. I'm here." Trent held her tightly.

Closing her eyes, Liza leaned her forehead against his chest and let the horror of the past few moments wash over and through her.

"It was Duke," she finally said. "He wanted to talk to me. Are you sure you didn't hit him?"

There was a long pause while she waited for Trent to respond.

"Duke Masonne?"

Though he made a sincere effort to hide it, Liza heard the skepticism in his voice.

"I told you I'd seen him. Now I've spoken to him." She couldn't see Trent's features in the darkness, but she could feel his body tense.

"Let's head back to the lights," Trent suggested, his arm around her shoulders and his hand on her arm. He pulled her hard against his side.

"Maybe we should…call someone," Liza said, uneasily conscious of the fact that in protecting her, Trent had fired his weapon and very likely put himself in line for disciplinary action.

"Who should we call?"

She wasn't certain. Not the police. Who? "An ambulance?" she offered.

"I didn't hit him. I'm positive. If I'd wanted to, I would have. By now, he's downriver. And judging from your last experience with Duke Masonne, it'll be another five years before you see him again."

Liza felt as if she'd been slapped. "Trent—"

"I'm sorry," he said. "That came out wrong. I was trying to put a humorous light on what just happened.

Let me tell you what I saw—a man chasing after you with his hand not clearly visible. When I got closer, you'd both stopped and you were begging him to leave you alone. He was doing something with his jacket. I couldn't see from behind, but I was afraid he was pulling out a gun, so I fired. Close enough to let him know I meant business but with room to spare."

"You missed him deliberately?"

"I didn't have a reason to shoot him. I just wanted to make your Duke Masonne look-alike hit the road. Did he say anything else? Some clue as to who he was?"

"Like what?" Liza felt the first traces of her temper. Trent was behaving as if she'd made up the entire incident, treating it as some flight of fancy or some sick way to handle delusions. "You saw him, Trent. You *shot* at him. It was Duke. Don't act like I'm having a hallucination or a nightmare. He was real. He was right there."

As they continued walking, Trent let the silence grow for a moment. "I saw a man, Liza. It was dark, and I was far enough away that I didn't get a clear look at him. But I heard you ask him to leave you alone and then beg him. Whatever he wanted, whoever he was, he's a man who needed to know that when a lady requests to be left alone, he should oblige."

Liza started to protest further, but she knew it was useless. Even if Trent had seen Duke, it would be hard for him to accept it. The accepted version of Duke Masonne's disappearance was that he was dead.

They'd made it back to a busier part of the levee, and in the distance Liza could see the bright lights of the French Market. She was suddenly aware that the black cat was no longer with her.

"Familiar." She turned and whirled, but the cat was gone without a trace.

"What?" Trent said.

"The cat. Did you see him?"

He shook his head. "I didn't see a cat." His smile was wry. "I'm not much good to you today, Liza. I didn't recognize Duke and I didn't see your kitty. You might have to trade me for a model with better eyesight." He brushed a strand of hair from her face. "But I did see you, and when I saw how frightened you were, I wanted to hurt that man, whoever he was."

Liza felt the brush of his fingertips on her skin. His touch was amazingly gentle, as it had always been for a man who lived such a rough-and-tumble life. In the two months she'd spent time with Trent Maxwell, he'd been an absolute gentleman. If she could have willed her heart to respond to him more fully, she would have.

"I can't undo the evening, but I can treat you to a wonderful dinner with some nice wine. You look so tired. It just makes me want to take care of you."

Liza swallowed. She wanted to say no. All she really wanted was to return to the levee and try to find a trace of Duke. She wanted physical evidence that he'd been there. That she'd seen him. That he was real.

And he was. Flesh and blood, not some apparition. He'd spoken to her. And he'd frightened her beyond rational thought. Why? What was it that she was so afraid of where Duke was concerned?

"Liza, what about dinner?"

"That would be lovely," she said, forcing a smile. Trent was trying hard to become important in her life.

He was a patient man who would defend her with his life. She knew she could do a lot worse.

"Maybe I should go back and look for the cat," she said, turning toward the river. She almost hoped that Duke would climb up the side of the levee and approach her now, where it was light and where there were other people who could see him clearly.

"There wasn't a cat in sight. He'll show up when he's ready. You know how independent cats are."

"Eleanor Curry left him with me. What if he's lost?"

"You aren't going to find that cat unless he wants to be found. I'll help you hunt tomorrow."

Liza felt a flush of anger. Trent was trying to be helpful, but... "Maybe I should just go home," she said softly.

"You shouldn't be alone right now. You've had a bad scare. What about Renaldo's? You like Italian."

"Fine," she agreed because it was the easiest thing to do. And because she didn't really want to go back to her home and spend the night alone.

*WELL, OUR APPARITION HAS physical form. He's the spitting image of all of those drawings hidden away in Liza's secret studio. Duke Masonne. The missing link in Liza's past. Well, well. He's a living, breathing humanoid with one helluva breaststroke in the mighty Mississip. I hate to abandon Miss Renoir, but I think my case will be better served if I follow this character.*

*I've deduced that he knows Liza, which indicates to me that he has a lot of explaining to do. Five years is a long time to be gone for a pack of cigarettes, as the old saying goes. But in the fading light of dusk, I could* detect a few changes in the physical exterior of our missing hero.

He's lost twenty pounds and toughened up. Where he used to be a desk jockey, he now makes a living in the elements. He's lost that polished, citified look.

And from the expression on his face when he looked at Liza, he doesn't mean her any harm. The plot thickens.

So where has he been and what's he doing back in New Orleans? Those are questions that will be answered only when I track him down. Which is exactly what I'm going to do.

I suppose those soft-shell crabs will have to wait. Just breathing this river air makes me want to wrestle a catfish to the deep fryer.

I hear him swimming. He's strong. Good endurance. Pretty soon, though, he should be climbing up the levee. Yep, here he comes. Not exactly the happiest humanoid I've ever encountered.

I'll just bet he's wondering who took two shots at him. A question I'd also like answered. He was obviously some friend of Liza's. Her current romantic interest, I'd guess. A man who carries a gun and uses it, so that makes him a law officer in all likelihood. He wasn't in a hurry to leave the scene of the shooting, so he must have reason to believe that if he's questioned, he has the right credentials.

Well, here comes the long-departed Duke Masonne. The river has left him chilled and dripping. So I'll follow him home and see what clues I can dredge up from his hideout.

If he's up to no good, then I'll have a chance to set up a few traps for him before he can do any more *damage to Miss Renoir. I'd say she's been hurt enough.*

*I hate to leave her without a hint of where I'm going, but perhaps I'll be able to deliver the goods on this guy. In the meantime, I have to say he's interesting. He's walking around dripping wet and acting as if it were an everyday occurrence. He's so good at it that he isn't even drawing attention. Hmmm. I'll have to study his technique. He just blends right in. And we're headed down Toulouse toward the heart of the French Quarter. The sun has gone down, the moon is out, and it's party time in "The City that Care Forgot."*

*Wow! I don't think Eleanor would like it if she knew I was traveling down Bourbon Street. Jazz, strippers, tap-dancing juveniles, and tourists all drinking that strange red drink in those tall glasses. I believe they're called Hurricanes, a New Orleans specialty. Man, humanoids partying en masse.*

*At last, though, we're turning down a quiet street. Pretty ritzy. So old Duke has some dough. Audubon Place. Very chic. I think maybe I'll have to take a look in his refrigerator before too much more time passes.*

## Chapter Four

Mike stepped out of the shower, his body warmed by the stinging spray but his heart still chilled by the events on the levee. Someone had shot at him. In the world of North Dakota where he'd spent the past five years, a weapon wasn't drawn except in self-defense or for protection.

Was he a threat to Liza Hawkins?

The only answer he had was in the newspaper clippings he'd read at the library. Nowhere had he caught even a hint of something that might explain what had just occurred. Or what had happened to him five years ago when he'd been so badly beaten.

He toweled himself dry and slipped into clean clothes. As he stepped out of the bathroom, he saw a black cat sitting in the doorway. It didn't seem possible, but it appeared to be the same cat that had been with Liza.

"Meow."

He stared at the animal.

"Meow." The cat walked toward him and brushed against his leg.

"Where the hell did you come from?" he asked,

wondering if he'd somehow slipped over the edge of sanity.

The cat didn't answer but walked toward the kitchen, one black paw batting at the refrigerator door.

"You're hungry?"

"Meow."

He opened the refrigerator and watched as the cat proceeded to check out his food, finally selecting a plate of leftover grilled tuna. Mike took it out and put it on the floor, watching as the cat began to eat.

"Glad to oblige," he said, still amazed. "At least one of us has an appetite." Food was the last thing on his mind. He walked to his apartment window, which looked out on a New Orleans street that might have been in one of Liza's paintings.

What had he done that might provoke someone to try to shoot him? And how good a shot was the shooter? Had he missed deliberately? Mike suspected that he had. The gunshots had been intended to drive him away, not mortally wound him. But why?

Duke Masonne had been a businessman. Successful, involved with the art world through Liza, a man who seemed to be solid and reputable. Seemed to be. That was the key phrase. Behind that facade there was something else, and Mike knew he had to dig it up no matter what it revealed about himself.

For the first time he understood Rachel Welch's reluctance about his need to explore the past. "Some things are better left alone," she told him, tears in her eyes as she'd watched him pack for the trip to New Orleans. "People change, Mike. Whatever was in the past, you've left it behind. Don't go walking back into it."

If he'd heeded her advice, he would be out in the

sharp April wind, birthing calves and drinking gallons
of hot coffee with Gabe and the other men. There had
been a sense of accomplishment in that life, a sense
of purpose that he'd lost since coming back to New
Orleans. Just as Rachel had warned, he'd stepped into
a quagmire. With each fact he uncovered, he felt himself sinking deeper and deeper into darkness.

It wasn't too late to leave. He could pack his bags,
board a plane and be back in North Dakota by morning. He knew Rachel and Gabe well enough to know
they'd never question him about what he'd discovered.
He could bury the past once and for all if he'd only
walk away.

The image of Liza appeared in his mind. He saw
her face, eyes wide with shock and fear. Even at the
memory, he felt his heart lurch. He wasn't sure what
the emotion was, but whatever it might be, it was too
strong to walk away from. He had to know the truth.
About Liza Hawkins and about himself.

"Meow."

He turned to find the cat staring at him with a look
filled with wisdom.

"She's worth the risk, isn't she?" he asked.

The cat nodded, one golden eye winking in agreement.

LIZA SAT AT THE TABLE in Renaldo's waiting for Trent
to return from the phone. He'd had to file a report
about the shooting, but he'd assured her it would take
only a few moments. She was glad for the time alone.

Her mind danced around the issue of what had just
happened. Duke Masonne had suddenly reappeared.
After five years, he'd emerged from the fading day-
light and spoken her name.

Or had he?

Her hands gripped the seat of her chair. "Please," she whispered. "Please don't let me be losing my mind."

It was her biggest fear. For five years, every night, she'd fantasized and dreamed of Duke's return. During the long afternoons when she'd sat in her private studio and drawn his features, she'd thought of what it would be like to see him again. She'd prayed for it.

But the reality was a far cry from anything she'd ever imagined. Instead of joy, the rush of love and happiness that she'd expected, she was terrified. Never in her life had she been more afraid.

The tears welled in her eyes and she blinked them away. Deep inside, she felt as if she'd been battered in a way that would never heal.

"Liza? Are you okay?"

She looked up to see Trent staring down at her. "Yes. Just a little unnerved, I suppose." She tried for a smile. "Are you sure that man wasn't hurt?" She couldn't bring herself to say Duke's name, especially since Trent had made it clear that he didn't believe it was Duke.

"The desk sergeant checked with the hospitals. No injuries reported. No bodies floating in the river." He smiled. "That's a joke. I told you I didn't hit him. If I'd meant to, he'd still be on the levee. Whoever he was, I doubt he'll be bothering you again."

She couldn't bring herself to say thanks. "I'm worried about the cat. I should go home and see if he's there."

"You're not hungry?"

She shook her head. "Honestly, I'm not. I'm sorry."

"Have a glass of wine and I'll take you home."

She nodded. "One glass." It would be simpler to concede than to argue. Renaldo's was safe, easy. Home might not be. She would be alone, left with her thoughts and her fears. She knew all too well that wasn't a good place to be.

"Trent, are you sure you didn't recognize Duke?" She knew better, but she couldn't leave it alone. She'd been honest with Trent from the very beginning. She'd told him about Duke and the past and how she was trapped in a hellish limbo of doubt about what had happened to the man she'd loved with all her heart.

"I didn't recognize him," Trent said with a gentle patience that made her feel even guiltier. "Remember, I never knew Duke. I didn't move to New Orleans until after he disappeared."

"But you've looked at the pictures."

"Which can never give a person a real sense of another human being. You know that. You're far better able to capture the essence of a person in your art. A camera captures the visual image. There's so much more to identifying a person."

Liza couldn't argue with that even though it wasn't what she wanted to hear.

Trent reached across the table and captured her hands. "Liza, whoever that man was, he meant to harm you. He pursued you into an isolated area. When you asked him to leave you alone, he didn't back off. He could see you were terrified. Hell, I was fifty yards behind him and I could see it. Yet he didn't back away. I know you want to believe it was the man from your past. But my theory is that he was someone who meant to harm you."

"And you made him stop," Liza said. From Trent's

point of view, he'd done the proper thing to save her. She had to acknowledge that. But something else was bothering her. "How did you know I was in danger?"

Trent squeezed her hands, then dropped them as the waiter brought two glasses and a bottle of wine. "Sip a little wine. It'll help settle your nerves."

Liza took a small swallow, amazed that it went down. Her throat felt as if a huge lump blocked it, and her chest was constricted. "Tell me. How did you know where to look for me?"

"There's something I want to tell you. I've debated about it, but now I think I have to."

Liza didn't think it was possible, but her level of dread increased. This was something she wasn't going to like. She could see it in Trent's eyes.

"I did a little poking around into the past. Since you've been so certain you've been seeing Duke Masonne hanging around, I decided to review his file." He hesitated, gaze dropping to the glass of wine he was swirling. "Liza, did you know Duke was a suspect in a murder?"

Liza stared at Trent. It was almost as if he'd suddenly begun to speak a foreign language. "He was what?"

"A suspect in a murder." Trent put down his wineglass and put both hands on the table. "This isn't the place to tell you." He waved a hand around at the busy restaurant.

"Finish it." Waiting would be far worse than hearing what Trent was about to say.

"Are you sure?"

"Just tell me." She sat perfectly erect in her chair, wineglass still in one hand.

"Before Masonne disappeared, a woman was murdered. Marcelle Ricco. Does the name mean anything to you?''

Liza shook her head while her mind searched frantically for some association with the name. ''Who was she?''

''Depends on who you ask. Some say she was a New Orleans socialite, a woman who was famous for her Garden District dinner parties and entertainments. Others say she was the madam for a ring of very high-class prostitutes. Sort of a Mayflower Madam, if you get the connection.''

Liza got it, loud and clear. ''And she was killed?''

''Her body was found the day Masonne disappeared. She was killed in her home.''

''And Duke is a suspect in her murder?''

''Yes.''

''Why? Why would he kill this woman? I've never heard of her.''

Trent motioned for her to sip her wine and waited until she'd done so.

''This isn't pleasant for me, please believe that.''

Liza wanted to scream. ''Just finish it. Please,'' she said, forcing her voice to remain calm, controlled. If Trent suspected how close to the breaking point she actually was, he'd quit talking and insist on taking her home. As it was, the buzz of activity around the restaurant sounded like white noise. She was totally focused on the man who sat across from her.

''There was some evidence that Masonne used Marcelle Ricco's services.''

''What?'' The one word escaped from Liza's lips in a rush of air.

''Not as a client himself, but as a...bonus for some of the men he did business with.''

"He sent his business associates to a madam?" Liza understood what Trent was saying, but it was so far-fetched that she was having difficulty comprehending it.

"That would appear to be the case."

"There were records, documents? How come no one told me?"

"There was no hard proof, but enough circumstantial evidence to lead the investigation in that direction."

Liza took another sip of wine, knowing that Trent was watching her closely. She had to keep her composure. And she had to ask the right questions.

"What kind of evidence?"

"The Ricco murder and Masonne's disappearance were two separate investigations. But the same people kept popping up in both. When the detectives began to question Masonne's business associates, Marcelle's name came up. More than once."

"But even if that were true, why would Duke kill her?"

"This is ugly, but it seems Marcelle was also running a small side business. Blackmail."

Liza digested that for a moment. "Even so, what could she blackmail Duke about? Even if he was using…sex as an incentive…" She faltered. It was so ugly. So dirty. And so untrue. The man she'd loved would never participate in that kind of business practice. That it was done by many other businesses she didn't doubt. But not Duke. He wasn't the kind of man who would trade in flesh for any reason. Her first impulse was to protest, but she realized instantly that to do so would cause Trent to stop talking.

"Masonne's business was based largely on his reputation as a keen businessman, a person of integrity and discretion. A scandal such as Marcelle could create would cause a lot of problems for him.''

"No doubt," Liza said, unable to keep the sarcasm out of her voice. "But to think he'd kill her. That's a stretch.''

Trent once again reached across the table for her hand. "I know this is hard for you to hear. But it's time you faced the truth about the past, Liza. If you don't, you'll forever remain a prisoner of it. I suppose I'm being selfish, but I want you to step into the present. The future. A future with me in it. And I'm not so stupid as to believe that I can share you, not even with a ghost.''

Liza had to force herself not to get up and flee. Her gut reaction was to run, to put as much distance between herself and Trent as she could. Her reaction wasn't fair, though. She wasn't running away from the man; she was trying to escape a view of the past that she found completely unacceptable.

How many hours had she spent in Duke Masonne's arms? She knew the most intimate facts about him. She knew how he reacted to her lightest touch, the feel of her lips on his skin. And he'd learned the secrets of her body. And each encounter had been special, a union of body and spirit that could never have been possible with a man who viewed a woman as something that could be bought and sold.

Images from the past spun in her head. Duke leaning over her in bed. Duke smiling at her as she woke up in the morning. Duke with a cup of fresh coffee and a kiss.

"I have to go home," she said, her voice barely a whisper.

"I knew this wasn't a good idea." Trent stood immediately, tossing money on the table for the wine. "My car isn't far from here. I'll get it."

"No, I'd like to walk," Liza insisted. "Would you just walk me home?"

For an answer, he took her arm and supported her as they stepped out into the darkened New Orleans street.

"I am sorry, Liza. But you had to—"

"Don't apologize. You didn't make up the past," Liza said. She tightened her grip on his arm for just a moment. "This has shaken me, but I had to hear it. I only wish someone had told me five years ago. Why didn't they?"

Trent turned her toward St. Ann Street. "Masonne disappeared and there wasn't enough conclusive evidence to pin the murder on him."

"Marcelle's murder was never solved?"

"Never."

"And her family? They still don't have an answer?" The thought of that was horrible. She knew what it was like to suffer in limbo.

"No one was ever arrested. And because Masonne wasn't officially a suspect, the department made certain not to trade in speculation or gossip. It wouldn't have been right."

"How did you find out about this?"

"I met one of the detectives in the gym last month. When you began seeing Masonne behind every bush and lamppost, I asked a few questions."

Liza kept walking. It was the only thing she could do.

"I know right now you don't believe any of this. That's a normal reaction. But think about it. Masonne's body was never found. There was no indication of foul play in his disappearance. Nothing disturbed at his business, no hint of a threat of any kind against him. The logical conclusion is that he disappeared because he wanted to, Liza.''

''But—''

''Let me finish. I don't think any of this negates the way he felt about you. I've come to know you fairly well. If you say the two of you were deeply in love, I believe that. One thing I've learned in police work is that people aren't black or white, good or evil. Masonne could have loved you with all his heart and still been involved with Marcelle. Smart people are always the most complex, and one thing we both agree on is that Duke Masonne was one highly intelligent man.''

Liza knew it was futile to argue. Trent was a man trained to draw conclusions from facts. That was one of the things about him that attracted her. He looked at real evidence and followed it in a straight line. He lived in a world of solid fact, unlike her own, which was founded on emotion, intuition and a strong belief in what she felt to be true.

Right now what she felt was at total odds with the facts Trent had laid out before her. The best policy, though, was to remain silent. If there was a grain of truth in Trent's allegations, she would think it through and decide for herself.

Trent stopped at the front door of LaTique Gallery and waited for her to unlock it. Liza knew he expected to follow her inside. Part of her wanted to have him with her, to hold the loneliness at bay. Even as she accepted her feelings, she was ashamed. Trent wasn't her father or older brother or fond friend she could use to keep the bogeyman away. He had fallen in love with her. He'd told her so. And if she couldn't reciprocate those feelings, it was time for her to stop leaning on him.

"I think I need some time to think about all of this," she said, gently placing a hand on his chest as they stood outside the gallery.

Trent shook his head and half turned away. "I knew you'd blame me. It's human nature to shoot the messenger."

"Wait," she said quickly. "I don't blame you. I only wish I'd known about this five years ago. I have to be honest with you, Trent. I owe you that much. I find it hard to believe that Duke was involved in any way with Marcelle Ricco." She saw he was about to speak and she put her fingertips on his mouth. "I don't want to believe it. But I know the police must have good reason to suspect him. All I'm saying is that if Duke were here right now, he could explain everything. In the end, he'd prove himself innocent."

Trent shook his head. "I only hope one day that you'll have that much faith and confidence in me."

His words were painful to Liza. She hadn't intended to hurt him, and yet she had. Perhaps she had nothing left to give to any man. Duke had taken all of her love, her heart. Maybe it would be best if she simply allowed Trent to move on to find someone capable of returning his love.

"I'm sorry," she said, tears welling in her eyes. "I know how hard this must be for you. Maybe you should give up on me, Trent. Maybe I am crazy or stuck in the past or…something."

"Maybe," he said, smiling a little. "But I'll take my chances. I've got enough of an ego to believe I can win you over to my side."

"Don't let me hurt you any more." Her emotions were mixed, her relief that he wasn't quitting bittersweet. "Good night," she whispered, standing on tiptoe to kiss Trent's lips before she slipped inside the gallery and locked the door.

She watched as Trent walked back the way they'd come to retrieve his car. His back was straight, his powerful shoulders squared. He was a handsome man, and a good one. Why couldn't she love him?

She turned away from the window, realizing that Trent had never answered her question about how he knew she was on the levee and in trouble. If he'd been checking up on Duke Masonne's past, then it was highly probable that he'd also gone hunting for her. It was probably just lucky circumstance that he'd seen her in the French Market and then had followed her when she'd begun to run away from Duke.

She was about to go upstairs to her apartment when she caught a glimpse of a fast black shadow darting toward the gallery door.

"Familiar." She couldn't believe it, but the black cat had returned. He'd found his way back to the gallery just as Trent had predicted. She unlocked the door and let him in.

*I DO BELIEVE I WAS promised soft-shells before the shooting incident and my adventure with Mr. Double Identity. The grilled tuna was an excellent appetizer, but I'm in the mood for a meal. It seems this case isn't going to be all that difficult to solve.*

*Yes, after an hour or so with Mike Davis, who is in actuality Duke Masonne, but who can't remember that tiny fact, I think the way to resolve this whole mess is a face-to-face between Miss Renoir and Mr. Double*

*Identity. One without guns and bullets. If they had only a moment to talk to each other, I think they could put the past behind them—the distant past and the immediate past. What comes through clearly from both of them is that they once loved each other, and I believe that love is so strong that it endures even now. I watched Duke Masonne watch Liza. It was as if he were drinking her into his pores. It was as if he'd been starving for years and she was the banquet. For two people who've been apart for so long, they have some intense emotions! E-yow!*

*The only monkey wrench in this project is the conversation I just overheard. Eavesdropped on, I should say. So Mike/Duke is a murder suspect in an unsolved murder. And the dead woman was someone who had a lot of secrets.*

*My immediate reaction to this—after spending a little time with Mike/Duke—is to wonder what kind of secrets this Marcelle Ricco might have had.*

*I'd be willing to stake my luxurious black kitty hide on the fact that Mike Davis is a decent, upright man. I've gotten pretty good at scoping out humanoids. Cats are a bit psychic, and as a feline sleuth, I've honed my sixth, seventh and eighth senses to the max. My gut tells me Mike is salt of the earth.*

*The thing that nags at me is that he doesn't remember who he used to be. There's one school of shrinkology that allows that when a person forgets, he has a reason to do so. In other words, Mike has deliberately buried Duke. I wonder if this is a form of suicide. Ah, a debate for a theologian at another time. Right now, I have a mystery to solve.*

*Liza is getting ready for bed. That leaves the pantry wide-open in another few minutes. While I'm sneaking* around, I'll try to figure out a way to get our two lovesick Homo sapiens to rendezvous while ascertaining the truth about Duke.

Marcelle Ricco. Now that's an excellent place to start. I guess, much as I hate to do it, I'm going to have to catch a streetcar and take a ride to the New Orleans Public Library.

Ah, Liza's hitting the sack. And she's crying. Well, maybe I have time for a few sandpaper tongue licks and whisker tickles before I snack.

There, there, little Liza. Oh, you're so appreciative of a big purr. And you're so warm and soft. Hmm, I suppose a nap wouldn't hurt. I always work better when I'm rested.

# Chapter Five

*The sheer white curtains billowed out from the windows on a breeze that smelled of spring rain. Liza opened her eyes in the darkness and inhaled, reveling in the scent of April, the promise of sun and flowers and the budding of new plants. Spring was her favorite time of year, when the light was slightly tinged with an electric green that made everything new and fresh. It was that light that she sought to capture in her paintings. The delicacy of it excited and inspired her. It was only in watercolors that she found she could come close to revealing it. When morning finally came, she would be out at dawn, easel and brushes in hand, to capture the moment of early light in the timeless city of New Orleans.*

*She got out of bed and went to the window to look out. For the French Quarter, the night was very quiet. Not even the partying sounds of Bourbon Street could be heard, just the soft chirrup of a cricket. It was almost as if she were all alone in the city.*

*At the thought of being alone, Liza crossed her arms and rubbed herself briskly. She was chilled. Tiny goose bumps tingled along her skin, making her smile at the memory of... Her smile disappeared. At the* memory of Duke Masonne. He was the one who'd told her that goose bumps were exterior symbols of a dance deficit. Whenever he saw them on her, he swept her into his arms for a moment of slow dancing.

Liza felt a sharp pain in her chest and wondered why. Then her gaze fell on the bed and she realized it was empty. Duke wasn't there. Hadn't been there for a long, long time. She was living on memories, nourished by dreams. Soon she would have to wake up and she didn't want to.

Suddenly afraid, she went to the small studio behind her bedroom. Flicking the switch that turned on the track lighting, she was confronted by dozens of portraits of Duke Masonne. Liza knew them all. She'd labored over them, making sure that each detail was accurate, each expression true to the man she loved.

She went to the first drawing and felt the horror bloom. It was covered in a blackish-red substance. She put her fingers in it, expecting to find that someone had thrown dark paint on her work. Someone had slipped into her home and destroyed her work! Her fingers brushed the drawing. When she pulled her hand back, it was coated in bright red blood.

Looking around, she saw that a second drawing had been slashed with a knife. It, too, wept blood. The paintings were bleeding!

Liza tried to back out of the room, but her body collided with something hard and warm. She whirled and found she was staring into dark eyes she'd once known. Brown eyes that had at one time held love for her now held something altogether different.

"He shouldn't have told you about Marcelle," Duke said. He lifted his hand and Liza saw the knife.

"Duke!" Liza reached out to touch his face, once

*so familiar and now so completely alien. Even his ex-*
*pression was a million degrees different. He jerked*
*away before she could touch him.*

"Duke, for God's sake!" *She stepped toward him*
*and he raised the knife.*

"I'm sorry, Liza," *he said.* "Now you know too*
*much."*

LIZA WOKE WITH A SCREAM tearing her throat. Beside
her, the black cat leaped to his feet, back arched and
hissing.

Finding the light switch to the bedside lamp, Liza
flooded the room with comforting illumination. It took
her a long time to believe the room was empty, but
when she was finally certain she was alone—except
for the cat—she got a grip on her breathing and slowly
felt her heart rate decrease. For a moment, it had
seemed that her heart would burst from her chest.

She felt something on her face and brushed a tear
away. She'd been crying in her sleep, weeping because
of the dream. Knowing she wouldn't be able to trust
another attempt at sleeping, she got out of bed and
went into the kitchen. Before long she had the kettle
going for a cup of tea.

When she passed the door to her private studio, she
didn't look at it. Even the thought of entering that
room had her heart racing again. It might have only
been a dream, but it had been so vivid. So intense.

So horribly painful.

She dropped the bag of herbal tea into a mug and
poured the hot water over it, waiting a few moments
for it to steep. While she waited, she went to the
kitchen window and looked out into the night. She

caught a whiff of honeysuckle, a scent so sweet and innocent that she felt tears threaten once again.

One spring evening, Duke had taken her to St. Martinville. They'd rented a small cottage on the Bayou Teche with a latticed front porch covered in honeysuckle. They'd lain in bed together, the sweet perfume of the wildflowers all around them, lulling them into gentle touches that ended in a passion so intimate, so powerful, that even at the memory, Liza began to pace the room.

By sheer will, she pushed the haunting images away. She had to leave the past behind. She had to. She'd lose her mind if she kept living on her hopes and memories. She didn't need a psychiatrist to tell her that. Even worse, now she was seeing Duke. The man on the levee had been real. She didn't doubt that. But had he really looked like Duke Masonne? The light had been poor, the distance great. He'd spoken her name and it *seemed* that he'd sounded like Duke. Only different. The inflection had been off.

Duke Masonne had lived an upper-class existence. Raised in New Orleans, he'd been to the best Catholic schools, had belonged to the right clubs. He'd spoken with a hint of French inflection, just the whisper of his heritage. The man on the levee had spoken with a flatter intonation.

Liza put lemon in her tea and took a sip. She'd *wanted* it to be Duke so badly that she'd seen what she'd hoped to see.

The truth she had to face was that if Duke Masonne was alive somewhere, he'd been gone for five years. He'd left her—deliberately abandoned her without even the kindness of a goodbye. He'd left her to live in a hell of not knowing, of imagining and worrying and wondering. The cruelty of such an act was beyond comprehension. If Duke was alive, then he wasn't the man she'd thought him to be. His love for her was a sham, which negated everything she felt for him.

Pascal was right. She could have the illusion of a pure love by clinging to the memory of a man long gone from her life, dreaming that he might one day miraculously reappear. Or she could accept that Duke had loved her and that something tragic had happened to him. He was gone. If he were alive, he would have contacted her long ago. She *had* to accept that he was dead.

And she had to quit seeing him in every stranger's face.

"Meow."

She picked up the black cat and snuggled her face into his fur. He was solid and real and offered comfort from her thoughts. "What am I going to do?" she whispered into his coat.

"Meow." He leaped out of her arms and went to the door of her studio. He scratched at the wood, demanding entrance.

"No," she said. "Not tonight. Let's wait until morning."

The cat only scratched harder. "Me-ow!" It was a demand.

Liza put her tea down and went to the door. The building she now owned was old, dating back to the 1700s. The doorknob was cut crystal, and she looked at it, reluctant to touch it and reawaken the frightening images of her dream.

"In the morning," she said, starting to turn away.

"Meow!" The cat slipped out a paw and snagged her bare foot, the claws just barely pricking her skin.

"Familiar!" she reprimanded him.

He batted the door again.

"For goodness' sake." She grasped the knob, turned it and swung open the door. With a swift movement, she switched on the track lighting and swept the room with her gaze. To her immense relief, all of her drawings were seemingly untouched. "See, it was only a dream." She spoke more to reassure herself than the cat.

Familiar bounded into the room and went straight to the table where her latest drawing waited to be finished. The black cat jumped up on the table and batted something with his paw.

Dread swept over Liza. She didn't know why, but she knew that the cat had found something that was going to upset her. Very slowly, she moved toward the table. She saw her ink pots, her pens and, finally, the antique silver pen. It was stuck straight into the drawing of Duke—dead center in his throat.

"No." She started to back away, but the cat's golden gaze caught her and held her. He stared deeply into her eyes, then gently batted the pen. "No," she said, shaking her head.

The antique pen had been Duke's gift to her, a rare instrument designed especially for Louis XIV, the pen that had allegedly been used by Frederico Milland when he drew the first sketches of the king's portrait. The pen, valued at close to twenty thousand dollars, had disappeared shortly before Duke. Liza had always assumed that someone visiting the gallery had stolen it. And now it was back.

"No," she said again, backing even farther away.

"Meow," Familiar insisted.

Liza finally understood. She looked around the

room and saw the sheer curtains at the end billowing on a sudden breeze. Whoever had put the pen on the table had entered through the window. It wasn't the most difficult feat in the world to climb the wrought ironwork that supported the balconies on both her second and third floors. The windows were walk-through, and though they were locked, they were also old.

She went to the window, closed it, then saw that the lock had indeed been broken. Something else was different in the room, and it took her a moment to realize what it was. The new picture she'd been working on, the one she'd started in acrylics, was destroyed. A smear of black paint obliterated the half-finished work.

The fear that touched her was very different from that which had come from the dream. Someone who knew a great deal about her past had entered her home and left a message. The pen was a clear symbol that, although she might have decided to put the past behind her, it wasn't solely her decision to make. The destruction of the painting seemed to say that her future was also completely out of her control.

She felt the cat brush against her legs and she scooped him into her arms.

"He's out there," she whispered to Familiar. "He's really out there. I'm not imagining this. But he isn't the man I loved and I don't know what he wants from me."

It wasn't even dawn, but Liza picked up the phone and dialed her manager's number. Pascal would know what she should do.

METHINKS I'VE *underestimated the situation. Yes, I was tired. Yes, I'd eaten two dinners and was deliciously full. But no way could I have slept through someone breaking the lock on the window and entering this apartment. No way.*

*Which means that the pen was put in this apartment sometime while Liza and I were both gone.*

*Much to my disappointment, that rules out Detective Trent as the prime suspect. He's good at showing up at just the right moment, as he did on the levee, but he can't be in two places at the same time. He was with Liza.*

*Now don't get me wrong. I have no reason to dislike the detective. Not really. I'm a little curious about why he withheld the information about Duke's possible involvement in a murder. Were I not such a cynical cat, I'd buy his story that he just found out. My suspicions run a little deeper, though. I think he's known this information for a while and he's chosen to use it now because it suits his purposes. Not exactly a criminal way to behave, but certainly manipulative. I just don't like the idea of Miss Renoir being emotionally used.*

*More troubling is that the culprit could easily be Mike/Duke. Man, I'm going to have to decide what to call him. He thinks of himself as Mike, but I know he's Duke. So is he the old man or the new? And did the old model actually have something to do with the death of Marcelle Ricco?*

*Let's stash that issue on the back burner and deal with the pen. Whoever left it did so this afternoon. It wasn't there yesterday, I'm certain of that. Whoever did it knew the value of the pen to Liza. I don't have a clue what it means yet, but I know it holds extreme significance based on her reaction to it. Probably emotional and financial—the dang thing looks old and old things are always expensive.*

The person who left the pen has some athletic ability. The wrought ironwork does offer a fairly fit person a method of gaining the balconies, and the window was something any average burglar could get through in three seconds flat. But this burglar brought something back instead of stealing.

The only possible motive was that he wanted to leave Liza a message she wouldn't miss. Judging from her expression, she got every syllable of it.

Nothing was disturbed, and the beautiful silver necklace with the lapis stone in it was left untouched on her desk.

So what is a black-cat detective to make of all these assorted observations? I'm puzzled, I must admit.

Mike/Duke didn't strike me as the kind of man who would terrorize Liza. He's obsessed with her, just as she is with him. And he's at a total loss to understand his connection to her. Why doesn't he remember? I think, perhaps, that's at the crux of this mess.

My only concern now is that he doesn't remember because maybe he did something so bad he can't face it. If I act as Cupid and bring these two lovesick humanoids together again, will I be responsible for putting Miss Renoir in the arms of a killer?

I have to know the answer to that before I can act as the agent of love that I've been known to be.

Ah, I think some fresh eggs and salmon over asparagus with a little hollandaise sauce is the ticket. A kitty needs a good breakfast to start the day. I do believe I see the sun peeping over the nearby rooftops. Another gorgeous spring day is announcing its arrival.

I need a plan, and it's something a little out of my league. I pride myself on my ability to judge bipeds. My acute sensibilities and my training have never *failed me—but in this case, I'm reluctant to trust my own judgment. There are times when a person is so troubled that they don't even know how badly off they are. This may be such a case. Mike/Duke has two lives, two personalities. Perhaps I'm seeing only the good side of him. I don't want to bring Dr. Jekyll and Mr. Hyde into Liza's life. I'm going to have to be very careful here.*

THE BUILDING THAT HAD once housed Masonne International was art deco in design, and looking at it, Mike was amazed that he'd ever inhabited such a building. When he went up to examine the bronze plaque that marked the entrance, he was even more shocked to discover that Duke Masonne had built the structure. *He'd* hired an architect and approved the design. Mike smiled at the whole idea. Out in North Dakota, there wasn't a single building that he knew of that even vaguely resembled this one. It was something to look at, especially since the early-morning rays of sunlight gave it a warm pink glow.

It was too early in the morning for anyone to be at work in the building, and Mike noticed that it was now a different business, owned by someone else. But his name was there, or his old name. Duke Masonne. It didn't sound like it had ever fitted him. Mike Davis was so much more solid, so much more…real.

He stepped back from the plaque and took one last look at the building. He hadn't come here to examine architecture. He'd come to find his past. Since Masonne International was no longer in existence, he'd have to get out the list of employees he'd dug up and set to work trying to track down someone who might talk to him. Someone who would talk to him and tell him the truth about what kind of man he'd once been.

He was about to leave when he heard a sharply indrawn breath. Slowly turning, he saw an older black man with a cart of cleaning supplies.

"Mr. Duke," the old man said, shaking his head in wonder. "They said you were dead."

Try as he might, Mike couldn't put a name to the man. He didn't remember him at all. "I *believe* I'm Duke Masonne," he said slowly, "but I can't remember anything about my past. Can you help me?"

The old man's eyes grew worried and he darted looks behind him. "If you don't remember, you better not stand around out here in the open. There's plenty of folks who *do* remember. And they remember all too well." He reached out and grabbed Mike's arm. "Come with me, and you'd better step lively before folks start comin' in to work."

Mike wanted to resist, but he sensed the man's sincerity. He allowed himself to be led behind the building and into a dark, alleylike entrance. Alert, he kept his gaze roving, on the lookout for an ambush. He'd already been shot at once. He didn't intend to make such an easy target the next time.

The old man led him to a small office with a kitchenette attached. He put on a pot of coffee and motioned for Mike to have a seat at the kitchen table.

"You don't even remember my name, do you?" the old man asked.

Mike searched his features, hoping for some clue. "No," he finally said.

"You built this little kitchen for me. You said I could live up here." Furrows appeared in the old man's forehead. "My name is Abraham. Abraham Brewer. You gave me a job."

"I don't remember," Mike admitted.

Abraham shook his head. "What happened to you? You disappeared and folks started sayin' you killed that woman. I knew it wasn't true, but the talk was all over the docks."

Mike felt as if he'd been slugged on the head. "Killed a woman? What are you talking about?"

Abraham's eyebrows rose until they almost touched his hairline. "My, oh, my, we've got some ground to cover, Mr. Duke. You got a lot of things to learn if you're gonna try and come back to this town."

Mike took a seat at the kitchen table where Abraham indicated. "Please, tell me what you're talking about," he said, knowing that he'd come too far to turn back now. Whatever he heard from Abraham was going to change his life forever.

"Lord, Mr. Duke, I hate to be the one to tell you all of this." Abraham cradled his mug of coffee in big hands.

Beyond his own dread, Mike felt a moment of pity for the man in front of him. "Of all the people who might have told me, I somehow think you're the best." He nodded. "You've already said you didn't believe I was guilty. Go ahead and tell me."

"It was that woman who kept asking you to import things for her. That rich woman from the Garden District. Had the big house. I delivered some things to her. Beautiful place. She was beautiful, too, but I knew she wasn't no good."

"What happened?" Mike prompted.

"The day you disappeared, they found her body. She'd been stabbed. Folks were saying that she entertained your business clients for you and that she tried to blackmail you. Lord, it would have broken Miss Liza's heart to hear such things about you.''

''I never saw any of this in the newspapers.'' Mike was having a difficult time believing the scandalous story. It sounded more like tabloid fare than anything related to life as he knew it.

''Wasn't in the papers. This was all talk. They never found enough evidence to put it in writing that you killed her. But the talk was all up and down the docks. Those of us who didn't believe it, we spoke up, but it didn't do no good. You were gone. No trace of what happened. That only made it look worse for you, if you know what I mean. Like you'd run off because you were guilty.''

Mike nodded. ''I can understand that.'' He hesitated. ''And Liza, did she believe I was guilty?'' No wonder she was terrified of him. If she thought he was a murderer, she had just cause to be afraid.

''I can't say what she knew,'' Abraham said. ''Once you were gone, she didn't come down here anymore.''

''I see.'' Mike didn't, but he knew if he thought about it, he'd begin to put the pieces together.

''Where did you go?'' Abraham asked. ''We all thought you were dead.'' There was a hint of resentment in the last statement.

''The first thing I remember is waking up in a hospital in North Dakota. I'd been beaten up pretty badly and I lost my memory.''

''What've you been doing?''

Mike grinned. ''Raising cattle.''

Abraham's eyes widened. ''You? On a horse? Mr. Duke, you couldn't even ride a bicycle proper. You were a swimmer, don't you remember?''

Mike shook his head. "And my name is Mike, not Duke. Mike Davis."

Abraham leaned closer. "No, you're Mr. Duke Masonne. It doesn't matter that you think you're somebody else. You're Mr. Masonne, and you'd better find out what happened to that woman or else when the po-lice find out you're alive, they're gone charge you with murder."

# Chapter Six

Pascal looked out of Liza's closet, his mouth dropping into a frown. "Put on some makeup, Liza. You're something of a celebrity. The days of being able to schlepp around like a bag lady are over. We can't afford to have people recognize you looking like you're about to be institutionalized."

"Pascal!" Liza found the strength to protest. Since he'd arrived, Pascal had made her strong coffee with chicory, forced her to eat buttered toast, and now he was determined to get her out of her apartment and "into the sunlight." All she wanted to do was talk about the antique pen, but Pascal was having none of that. At least not until she'd gotten dressed and was outside. That was the carrot he was dangling in front of her.

"Really, Liza. After years of being a nonentity, you should relish the idea that people will recognize you. Dress the part! It's how careers are built. I've worked like a field hand to get this for you. Please, please, don't ruin it."

Liza took the red dress he handed her and went into the bathroom to don it and apply makeup. One glance at herself in the mirror and she saw why Pascal was so upset. She looked awful! Her hair was a tangled mess and her skin was so pale she could have consumption.

In a few moments, she was dressed and her cheeks had a healthy glow—thanks to blusher. As much as she sometimes resented Pascal's bossiness and micromanagement, she had to admit that he knew how to keep her from dwelling on the things that tormented her.

"A stroll around Jackson Square and then brunch," Pascal said, offering his arm. "You look splendid. That red dress contradicts your paleness. Gives you that artistic élan."

Liza rolled her eyes. She made sure the black cat was with her as she stepped into the street. "We have to go where Familiar can sit with us," she warned Pascal.

He gave the cat a dirty look. "If you insist. You know I don't approve of animals living inside."

Liza laughed. "Familiar is the only thing that's kept me from having a breakdown. You'd better be exceptionally kind to him, Pascal. If he has to go home, you'll have to sleep at the foot of my bed."

"I'm suddenly elated," Pascal said drolly. "This is the first time in five years you've even mentioned the possibility of someone sleeping in your bed. Even if it is only as a foot warmer, I'll take that as progress. You've been alone far too long. At last, the ghost of Duke Masonne is being pushed aside."

Liza gently extracted her arm from his. "I need to talk to you about Duke. Now," she said, ignoring the piercing look he shot her. "Something's happened. Aside from the fright I got when I found that antique pen."

"Let's stroll," Pascal said. "I have a feeling this is a subject that would be best broached in the warmth of the sun."

Liza didn't disagree and she waited until they'd walked to Jackson Square to begin. Indicating a bench in the park surrounded by the vivid hues of pink and purple azaleas, she waited until Pascal was looking at her. She wanted to monitor his expressions. Familiar jumped up onto the bench between them and began cleaning his front paws. She stroked the cat a moment before she began to talk.

"Trent told me yesterday that Duke is…was a suspect in a murder. Did you know this?"

Pascal bit his bottom lip. "Yes, I did."

"Why didn't you tell me?" Liza kept a careful rein on her anger. This wasn't the first time that Pascal had assumed more control of her life than was appropriate. They'd argued about it often—and violently. It didn't matter that he was trying to protect her. He had no right to do such things.

"What good would it have done for you to know?"

"That's not your call," Liza said pointedly. "I had a right to know."

"Duke was gone. He'd vanished. Would knowing he might have killed a woman made it any easier?"

Liza stared into Pascal's pale blue eyes. He refused to back down and that, at least, made her less angry. He'd acted in what he thought were her best interests, and he still believed his actions were valid.

"I don't know. Pascal, it isn't your job to make my life easier. Your job is to sell my work."

"I can only sell it if you paint it. Remember, Liza, you didn't paint for nine months after Duke disappeared. If you'd thought him a murderer, you might not have painted for years. You were on the verge of a breakdown. Deny it, if you can.''

She knew he spoke the truth. The problem was that although she saw his point for doing what he did, she didn't like it. ''This woman, Marcelle Ricco, what do you know about her?''

''She was a very big fan of your work.''

''What?'' Liza searched Pascal's eyes to see if this was his idea of a sick joke. She saw instantly that he wasn't kidding.

''She bought several of your paintings. Remember the one of the little girl on the front porch? That was one of her favorites.''

Liza remembered the painting well. It was also one of her favorites and had been the first painting she'd sold for five figures.

''Marcelle was a woman of exquisite taste,'' Pascal continued. ''A beautiful woman. And her entertainments were always the height of fashion. There was no telling who might appear. A rock star, a televangelist. There was always the element of the unexpected, which made the party a smashing success.''

''You attended them?'' Liza was astonished. Pascal moved in many social circles—it was a big part of his effectiveness at getting his clients known—but she'd never expected he would have socialized with Marcelle Ricco.

''Whenever I got an invitation. Marcelle knew the art of a restricted guest list that constantly evolves. One moment you'd be on the list and the next you'd be dropped to make room for someone else. There was no malice in it. She was just a very calculating hostess who knew how to keep her parties fresh and her invitations sought after.''

"I understood she was a…" Liza balked at the word. "That she provided women for men."

To her surprise, Pascal laughed. "Liza dearest, you act positively provincial."

She ignored his teasing. "Is it true?"

"In the strictest sense, yes. But it wasn't like a Wild West saloon." He was still chuckling.

Liza finally lost her temper. "Duke was suspected of killing her, Pascal. It isn't funny."

He sobered instantly. "Of course not. I'm sorry."

"Do you know if he really had…dealings with her?"

He thought for a moment. "No. I never saw him at her parties. But then, I wasn't invited to all of them. Duke Masonne's world was international. Many cultures view that sort of thing very differently than you do."

It wasn't what Liza wanted to hear. "I don't believe it."

Pascal shrugged. "I can't say either way." He motioned for her to stand up. "Let's walk," he said.

Around them, the French Quarter was coming to life as tarot-card readers and artists began to set up their booths around the square.

"Now tell me about finding the pen," he prompted as he led her toward La Madeleine, a café specializing in fresh-baked pastries and breads. "We'll have some breakfast and see if we can't figure this out."

"I had a bad dream, and when I woke up, Familiar insisted on going into my private studio." She looked to make sure the cat was following them. He was two steps behind, his attention shifting from side to side as if he were actually protecting her, Liza thought. She continued with her account. "When I looked on the desk, the pen was there, just as it was when you looked at it. And then I noticed that my new work was destroyed.''

''Just the new painting?''

''Yes, the one I told you about. It was as if whoever did this thing didn't like the idea that I was changing. Almost as if he...'' She hesitated.

''Wanted to keep you in the past?''

Liza understood the implication in Pascal's statement and she didn't have an answer. After a moment, he spoke again.

''Is it possible that pen could have been somewhere on the desk? Tucked under some books or in a crevice in the back? That desk is old, you know.''

''No.'' Liza was adamant. ''The pen disappeared about the time Duke did.'' It was something that had always troubled her. ''I searched for it for months and then gave up. Duke gave it to me, remember?''

''Yes, I remember very well. It was an extraordinary gesture.'' Pascal's normally cheerful face was troubled. ''Who else knew the significance of that pen?''

Liza thought for a moment as they walked beneath the shady oaks. ''I can't say. I was so excited I told several of my friends.'' She gave a wry smile. ''But I haven't talked to them in a while. As you know, I've lost contact with so many of the people Duke and I knew together. It was just too painful. It didn't matter that no one asked me what had happened to Duke. It was what everyone was thinking.''

''Yes, I know. And you say the window was open and the lock broken?''

''Yes.''

''I don't want you to be angry with me, but I took the liberty of calling Trent while you were bathing.

Some of his men are going to examine your apartment.''

The chill that touched Liza was like a blast of arctic air. ''You called the police? They're in my private studio? My drawings—the police shouldn't be in there. That work is private.'' The panic was almost worse than her earlier fear.

''They'll be finished before we get back. I knew how distressing it would be for you to have to watch them examine your home. That's why I insisted that we leave. And Trent assured me that he would safeguard your privacy.'' He grasped her arm and gave it a shake. ''Liza, this has to be done. We have to find out who's tormenting you in this way. This was an act of violence, a threat to your safety. It must be stopped.''

''Trent shouldn't see those drawings.''

''Lisa, it will be okay.''

''I don't want to believe someone really broke into my home.'' The idea was an abomination. Someone had been among her things, had touched her possessions, looked upon things that were intimate and personal and reserved only for herself. It was a feeling of the deepest violation.

''Liza, when I spoke with Trent, he told me about the man following you. I don't want to alarm you, but I'm very worried about all of this.''

''Me, too,'' Liza agreed.

Pascal shook his head. ''I think I'm worried in a different way.'' His mouth hardened into a thin line. ''And for a different reason.''

''Because you believe Duke did something wrong?''

For a long moment, Pascal's light blue gaze held

hers. "I'm not certain about that. But if he *is* alive and back in New Orleans, then I do believe he was involved in something bad. Otherwise, why leave the way he did? If you think about it honestly, you'll agree that nothing can redeem the way he left. It's a terrible catch-22 for you, Liza. If he's alive, he's not a very nice man. If he's dead, then someone is trying to mess around with your mind. Someone very sinister."

"Why? Why would anyone do such a cruel and awful thing?" Liza demanded.

Pascal took her left hand and held it. "You're about to become very famous. Fame excites envy. It wouldn't be difficult for someone to delve into your past. Some sick individual might see an opportunity to cause you mischief."

Liza suddenly felt nauseous. The very idea that someone might concoct such an elaborate scheme as to pretend to be Duke, to break into her home and leave a valuable and sentimental object—not to mention destroying her work—it was sickening.

"But what about the pen?" she asked, suddenly thinking of its value. "How would they know about it and where would they get it?"

Pascal shrugged. "Let's wait and see what the police report shows," he suggested.

"No. Where would they get the pen?" He was dodging her question, and that made her uneasy.

"I don't have an answer and you wouldn't like the supposition I'm drawing. The pen and Duke disappeared near the same time. Now they have both returned," he said.

"You think Duke did such a thing, stabbing the pen through his own picture?" Liza didn't believe the level of dread such a possibility evoked. "You really believe this?"

"I don't know what I believe. We don't have enough information. But we will, I promise you that."

*LIZA HAS HIT UPON the one big question in the entire episode. The pen is valuable. What kind of thief breaks into a house to leave something of value? I don't think Robin Hood has moved out of Sherwood Forest and into New Orleans.*

*I'm curious to hear the police report myself. Someone broke in or someone set it up to look like a very convincing break-in. I'm trying to remember exactly what I heard that made me insist on investigating that room. Liza was distressed, waking up from a nightmare, but at the time I didn't know what her dream was about. Still, I was compelled to go into that room. And the strangest thing is that my keen kitty hearing wasn't alerted at all. It was almost as if… Liza isn't careless. She locks her doors and windows. I've watched her check them all before.*

*I must have heard something. It's all here, buried in my kitty subconscious. I wonder if a swinging watch could put me under and my dark side could be explored.*

*Nah! I've been studying the bipeds too much. Kitties don't have a dark subconscious. But humanoids sure do. Thank goodness I know that the man following Liza around is really Duke Masonne even though he doesn't know what that means. The simplest solution would be for Duke and Liza to meet and talk. She has answers that he needs, and his presence would put so many of her nightmares to rest. But what if Duke is off his rocker and is stalking Liza? What if I'm the instrument of their meeting and it all goes awry?*

*But I've never been wrong in matters of the heart. I suppose I'll just have to trust in my own judgment. I'd better get to work if I'm going to set up a meeting between the two. The way things look now, Duke will be behind bars and Liza will be too afraid of him to even risk a conversation.*

*As for all of this Marcelle Ricco business, I simply can't believe that Mike/Duke was involved in a cold-blooded murder. The man I met as Mike doesn't seem the type who'd be involved with a woman who ran a "for hire" business. Of course, Mike has been shaped by an entirely different set of environmental factors than Duke. Hmmm, too bad I don't know any clinical psychologists. I think this might be the definitive case of environment versus genetics.*

*I think I'll stroll back to the apartment and check on the progress of the police. First, I want to get Liza's attention and let her know what I want off the menu. Yes, she's following my paw. Right down to the ham-stuffed croissant. Ah, she understands that I want it and that I'm leaving.*

*If a black cat could blush, I certainly would. The long-legged artist just took me on her lap and gave me a kiss, right in front of God and everybody. I don't know if Mike/Duke is the man for her, but if he is, he's one lucky, lucky guy.*

MIKE STOOD AT THE CORNER and watched as two policemen came out the windows of Liza's second- and third-floor balconies and began to inspect all the window casings. There had obviously been a break-in. What troubled Mike was that he hadn't caught a glimpse of Liza. Was it possible someone had hurt her? He started forward and then caught himself. What was he going to do, demand that they tell him what had happened?

The end result would be his arrest. He was a suspect in an unsolved murder, according to Abraham. He was still reeling from that turn of events. He'd thought that maybe Liza could help him clear up the issue. Now, though, he was beginning to see that more was happening in Liza's life than he'd first suspected. A lot more.

He heard her voice before he saw her and just had time to duck down a narrow alley before she passed by on the arm of a man who looked vaguely familiar. Mike's heart began to race at the thought that he might recognize someone, but then he remembered he'd looked at a lot of newspaper articles. More than likely he recognized the man from them, not from any memory.

"Pascal, the police are still in my apartment." Liza stopped in front of the alley and pointed up to the uniformed officer dusting for prints outside her second-story window.

"So sorry. Trent assured me they'd be gone in an hour. I suppose everything took longer. Let's walk down to that little boutique with the lace gowns and hats. I know you've forgotten, but you have a show tonight in the Fine Arts Museum of St. Charles. I think you need something new to wear. Something for spring and for success."

"I don't feel like shopping," Liza said. She hesitated on the street.

For a moment, Mike felt as if he'd touched an electric fence. The current tingled through him as Liza shifted and looked toward him almost as if she could sense his presence. He waited breathlessly as she turned and swept her gaze down the alley.

To his surprise, the black cat came out of nowhere and gave a loud meow just inches from where he stood.

Liza broke free of her companion and stepped toward the cat. "Familiar, you want to go shopping?" she asked. She held up a bag. "I have your ham croissant."

"Meow." Familiar darted back deeper into the alley.

"Leave the cat," Pascal said in an annoyed voice. "You've become as obsessive about him as you are about Duke. That damn animal is nothing but trouble."

"Just a minute," Liza insisted, stepping farther into the shadows of the alley. "I'll just take him up to the apartment. Besides, I suppose I should see what they've done to my place."

Mike thought his heart couldn't possibly beat any faster. It wasn't the fear of discovery; it was that Liza was only ten feet away from him. Even in the dimness of the alley, her beauty seemed to glow. She was too pale, though. And the dark circles beneath her eyes made him want to reach out and pull her into his arms. To hold her and comfort her.

"Familiar," she said. "Come on, kitty, kitty. Mean old Pascal is getting angry. Come on. I don't want to leave you wandering the streets. Anyone could catnap you."

To Mike's surprise, the black cat that had been in his apartment came right up to his leg and sat down.

The cat was leading Liza to him. But he had to be very careful not to startle her too badly.

When she was only six feet away and had almost reached the cat, Mike bent down and picked Familiar up.

"Liza," he said softly, "I won't hurt you. Please."

He saw the fear sweep across her face.

"Duke," she said, her voice a whisper, "is it really you?"

"I have to talk to you," Mike insisted. "Will you meet me?"

He saw her begin to back away and knew he had to say something that would make her believe him. If only he could think of one thing from the past that would cement the bond that had once been between them. But the past was a black void. No matter how he tried to force them, the memories failed to return.

"My name is Mike Davis," he finally said. "Or at least that's the name I've used for five years. I don't know who I really am, but a lot of people seem to think I'm Duke Masonne."

That stopped her, and she was listening.

"Liza, let that confounded cat go!" Pascal called from the sidewalk. "It's hot standing here in the sun."

"I'm coming. Just a moment."

Mike was amazed that Liza was able to sound so normal. And she wasn't running away. She was actually standing within a few feet of him, her golden-brown gaze riveted on his face. It was almost as if she were touching him.

"Duke, where have you been?" Liza asked softly.

"I don't know a lot about the past. I've been in North Dakota for five years. I was injured. Severely. Someone beat me up and left me in a boxcar. When

I came to, I was in a hospital and I couldn't remember anything about my past. Not even my name.''

He saw the compassion flicker across her face, but then it was replaced by coldness.

"Why should I believe you? How did you happen to remember my name?"

He reached into the pocket of his shirt and pulled out the business card that was now worn and tattered. "This is what I was trying to give you on the levee. It was the only thing they found on me when they brought me to the hospital." He handed it over to her.

While she was reading it, the man on the street yelled out again. "I'm coming in to get you, Liza. And I'm calling the animal control on that damn cat. Enough is enough. Quit acting like a child and hurry up. The cat can take care of himself."

"I'm coming." Liza looked up from the card. For long seconds, she didn't say anything. "Meet me tonight, at midnight. Beside the statue of Andrew Jackson in the square."

"At midnight," Mike answered, feeling as if he'd suddenly been given the gift of a lifetime.

"I have to go." She handed the card back.

"I'll take care of the cat," Mike offered. He owed the black devil a real treat.

Liza handed him the bag with the sandwich. "See to it that he's well treated," she said.

"Liza!" Pascal didn't bother to hide his growing annoyance.

Liza whirled and ran back down the alley, her golden curls catching a slanting ray of morning light just as she turned the corner and disappeared.

## Chapter Seven

Liza concentrated on keeping the expression on her face neutral as she met Pascal's scowl. "The cat belongs to a friend of mine," she reminded him. "I'm responsible for his safety. I had to try to catch him."

"So where is the black devil?"

"He wouldn't come to me, but he wanted the sandwich, so I left it for him. Since he's right across the street from the apartment, I think he'll be safe." Liza was so relieved to have the cat to draw Pascal's attention that she found she was babbling.

"That cat doesn't have enough sense to come in out of the rain. The only good thing is that if something should happen to him, there are hundreds of black cats around. I could replace him and you'd never know."

"Oh, I'd know," Liza said, though her tone wasn't argumentative. She'd finally calmed her heart rate and got her breathing under control. She'd spoken with *Duke*. She'd actually talked to him. He had a reason for not calling her, for disappearing for five years, for breaking her heart. He'd lost his memory. It was an astonishing revelation, but the only one that would explain five years of silence.

She stumbled over a broken piece of sidewalk, almost falling. Pascal caught her arm just in time.

"Be careful," he warned. "You could break an arm. The demand for your work is growing rapidly. An injury could be very damaging to your career."

Liza only smiled. "Not today," she said. She gave him a dazzling smile. "We have to find the perfect dress for tonight." Something that would go well with the beautiful silver-and-lapis necklace that Duke had given her, though she didn't say that out loud. Pascal hated the necklace, saying it was dated and old-fashioned. Not the image she needed to create as an up-and-coming artist. But it was the gift that had sealed their agreement to marry, and since it had been crafted by his grandmother, it might be the one thing that would reawaken his memory.

"You seem awfully chipper all of a sudden," Pascal said, his eyes narrowing in suspicion. "What happened? Did you meet Santa Claus in that alley?"

"No," Liza said, laughing. It seemed that it had been years since she'd actually laughed out loud. "It's that cat. You may think he's ordinary, but he isn't. He's very, very special." It was the cat that had somehow known to lure her into the alley. The whole thing was just perfectly extraordinary. "Here's the boutique. And look at that silk dress in the window—it's perfect." The black silk sheath was shot through with brilliant threads of cobalt and silver.

Pascal gave her another searching look. "You're enthused over a dress? Normally, I have to select your clothes. You'd just as soon wear a flour sack."

"No, really, that dress speaks to me," Liza said, pushing open the door. "I'm going to buy it if it fits." She had fourteen hours to wait until midnight. Fourteen long hours during which she'd be deviled by her common sense and tormented by what ifs. Duke Masonne, after an absence of five years, had suddenly reappeared. He was a suspect in a murder. His only defense was that he didn't remember a thing. A cynical person would observe that his was certainly a convenient forgetfulness. But Liza didn't want to be cynical. She didn't want to think too hard about her plan to meet Duke at midnight. All she wanted was for the time to pass and for her to be in the sweet darkness of the square—with Duke.

"As soon as we finish, I'm going back to that alley to find out what you stumbled into. Whatever it is, I want a supply of it. I've never seen you so tractable."

"Don't push your luck," Liza said, unable to stop smiling. "Come on, let's shop." The clerk she signaled slipped the dress off the mannequin and Liza hurried into the dressing room to try it on.

MIKE, SANDWICH BAG IN HAND and cat following, started back to his apartment. His encounter with Liza had happened so fast that it was difficult to believe it had actually occurred. But it had. And in a matter of fourteen hours, he'd be meeting with her again.

Midnight in the square. Something far back in his brain stirred. There was some significance to that meeting place, that time. If only he could remember what.

In the five years he'd spent learning the cattle business, he'd often thought about what his past might be. During the long nights on the range, he'd wondered what kind of life he might have led. Nowhere in his wildest fantasies had there been a woman like Liza Hawkins. Strange, but when he'd imagined himself in different places, he'd never thought to imagine a woman in his life.

Was it because no fantasy creation could measure up to the real woman with whom he'd had a relationship?

Liza Hawkins. He reached into his pocket and felt the worn card that had been his only link with the past. If he hadn't come back to New Orleans, he'd never have known anything about Liza.

"Meow!"

He looked down to see the cat burred up at his feet. Momentarily disoriented, Mike looked around to discover he was in a section of the French Quarter known as Pirates Alley. The cobbled street ran between the cathedral and several old brick buildings that served as homes. Although the alley was well maintained and beautifully landscaped with flowering mimosa trees and fronds, it was still deserted.

The cat was peering straight into a thicket of huge elephant ears, back arched and hissing.

Mike stopped, listening for the sound of a dog or some other creature that might have caused the cat to behave so strangely. Though the sounds of the city were all around him, the alley was quiet. Unnaturally quiet.

He had two choices—he could continue forward or retreat.

The cat made the decision for him. Growling, he began to back away. Mike remembered he'd already been shot at. He was unarmed and a suspect in a five-year-old murder. The one thing he didn't need right now was trouble.

Discretion was the better part of valor in this instance. Following the cat, he withdrew, returning to

Royal Street and the bustle of the French Quarter crowds.

After he'd gone a block, he pulled into the nook of an antique store with a good view of the street and waited. Several minutes passed before a man emerged from the alley. He looked in neither direction, but turned right.

With the cat at his heels, Mike followed. He wasn't in the least surprised when the man stopped at LaTique Gallery and went inside.

For a long moment, Mike watched the building where Liza lived and worked. Although he tried hard to dismiss the idea, it was already planted. Had Liza called someone and told them about their meeting in the alley? Had he been followed? Had her willingness to meet him been an act?

"Meow," the cat said. His golden eyes seemed to be watching Mike with an intensity that was a little unnerving.

"I have an appointment," Mike said, looking at his watch. Now it was more important than ever to meet Kyle LaRue, one of his former employees, at least according to Abraham. The janitor had set up the appointment for Mike, saying that Kyle had once been a trusted friend and was someone who could shed some light on Duke Masonne's past.

"Meow." The cat rubbed against his leg once, then darted across the street to LaTique Gallery.

Mike felt a strange satisfaction that the black cat would be waiting there when Liza returned. There was something about the cat that inspired his confidence. What was it Liza had called him? Familiar. The perfect name. "Keep an eye on her for me," Mike said

softly as he watched the cat slip through the open door
as a policeman made his exit.

*MIKE/DUKE DIDN'T SEE the man in Pirates Alley, but I
did. Old Trent makes another appearance. I'm beginning to view this NOPD detective as a loose cannon—
and one with a deadly load. True, he could have killed
Mike/Duke on the levee and he didn't. But he was
awfully quick to draw his weapon and fire. I think it's
my duty to try to find out a few things about Trent
Maxwell.*

*So the fingerprint experts have finished. If I stand
around, maybe I can hear the report. The scene of the
crime is always the best place to pick up the real facts.*

*Yes, just as I suspected. No fingerprints other than
Liza's on the window casements. No prints at all on
the pen. Trent is thanking all the officers involved. It
looks like the show is over for the moment.*

*No one is saying it, but the general attitude is that
the broken lock could have happened any time. As for
the destruction of the half-finished painting and the
fact that a pen missing for five years was stuck into a
drawing—the police are acting as if this is merely a
case of female hysteria, especially since she's an artist
and has been "seeing" a dead man for the past five
weeks. This is common knowledge among the policemen. Very neat setup if you ask me. Reminds me of a
Bette Davis classic,* Hush...Hush, Sweet Charlotte.

*Now the question is, who would want to set Liza up
as mentally unstable, and why? I now have a three-
pronged investigation. Who savagely beat Duke Masonne five years ago? Who murdered Marcelle Ricco?
And why would Trent Maxwell allow his co-workers
to act as if Liza were unstable?*

*For a case that originally looked simple, this has gotten to be a real web of deceit. The duplicity of humanoids is always amazing, and perfect fodder for the razor-sharp brain of Familiar, Feline Detective. Sherlock Holmes, eat your heart out. Once I find a biographer to record my cases, I'll have my own book and television series.*

LIZA ADDED A NEW PAIR of shoes to the stack of packages Pascal was carrying for her. Normally, he had to threaten her into shopping, but today she'd turned the tables. He was thoroughly sick of watching her select clothes. Liza knew she was simply staying as busy as possible so that she wouldn't have time to think.

Thank goodness the day was almost over. They'd shopped and eaten and talked until it was nearly six o'clock. It was finally time for her to go home, get ready for the opening, then count the minutes until midnight.

"You've been a doll," she said to Pascal as she led the way back to her building.

"Just take a hot bath and look beautiful tonight. The newspaper is sending a photographer, and I'm hoping several of the television stations will also come."

"Have I thanked you lately?" Liza asked. She was as appreciative of his sour company as she was his efforts in building her career. Pascal wasn't an easy man to get along with—he was bossy and domineering. But he was also a loyal friend. Ever since Duke had disappeared, he'd played a bigger and bigger role in her life, taking over completely the selling of her paintings and the burden of her finances.

"Liza, you know I'm not pressuring you, but over seventy percent of your work has already been sold.

We need something new. Any plans to paint more watercolors? It's been…a while.''

Pascal had never been a master of understatement, but now he was trying hard to be subtle. She hadn't worked in several weeks—ever since she'd begun to see Duke. *And it hadn't been her imagination.* Fear that she might be losing her mind had impacted her ability to paint, but now…

''I'm starting to paint tomorrow,'' she said casually. ''I have an idea. Something new.''

''You know the watercolors are where you've made your name?''

Pascal's immediate concern made her smile. ''I know. You've already lectured me soundly about the importance of staying with my current style until my audience is well established. I intend to follow that advice.''

''Thank goodness. You aren't always the easiest artist I've ever worked with to guide, you know.''

''One of my greatest attributes. I'm hard to guide.'' Liza was only gently teasing him.

''So what's the new idea?'' Pascal asked.

''Remember the day I told you about when I was sitting in Jackson Square drinking a café mocha and saw that man coming out of an apartment with a painting and later, on the news, I found out it was an art theft in progress?''

''Yes.'' The word held more than an edge of criticism. ''Acrylics and a new attitude. Fantasy, I believe, is what you called it. Maybe you could draw crime scenes for the police.'' He hesitated. ''I don't like it and neither will your audience.''

''That was the painting the intruder destroyed,'' Liza reminded him. ''The idea of it intrigues me.

You're always telling me that I should paint what appeals to me. If it doesn't work, I'll paint something else.''

"An artist has to continue to experiment, to grow," Pascal said. "Just don't get hung up if it doesn't work."

"I won't." She gave him a sidelong glance. "I can tell you don't like the idea, but at least you aren't having a fit."

"Just work, Liza. The finished product will do all the talking. Now let's stow these packages. We both have to get ready for tonight."

"Oh, yes," Liza said. "Tonight."

MIKE ENTERED THE DARK BAR and stood for a moment, getting his bearings. It didn't seem to be the kind of place he'd frequent, but who knew what he'd been like when he was Duke Masonne. The idea that he'd once been someone else—someone very different—had begun to sink in and he'd felt the need to search for things that seemed familiar. But if The Python Pit was the kind of bar that was part of his past, he wasn't certain he really wanted to regain his memory.

The place was almost empty. A couple sat at a table, so intent on each other they never even noticed his arrival. And a solitary man sat at the bar, watching Mike in the mirror with an expression on his face that told Mike who he was. Kyle LaRue.

There was nothing about the man that seemed familiar. It was the amazed and slightly fearful expression on Kyle's face that Mike recognized. Here was someone who'd known him in the past—someone who'd thought he was dead.

As he walked toward the bar, the man slipped from his stool and stood. Mike noticed that he was wearing an expensive suit and looked as out of place in The Python Pit as Mike felt.

"My God, it is you," the man said. "I thought old Abraham was finally going senile. I almost didn't come today."

"I know your name, and Abraham says we were once friends." Mike shook his head. "I'm afraid I can't remember."

Kyle nodded. "Amnesia. That's what Abraham said. You don't have a clue about anything." He watched Mike for a moment, a look of indecision on his face. Finally, he motioned to a booth. "Let's sit over there. It'll be a little more private."

When they were seated, Mike smiled at the intense scrutiny of the other man. "Have I changed?"

"Not so much physically. The Duke Masonne I knew was trimmed, starched and always elegantly attired. You're a little more casual."

"I've been working on a cattle ranch. Starched and elegant aren't exactly part of that lifestyle."

Kyle laughed out loud and seemed to relax a little. "Well, the new look suits you. There's still that military posture underneath the flannel. I suppose your body remembers certain things even if your mind doesn't."

"That's an interesting supposition." For just a flash, Mike had the memory of Liza's lips on his. It was so sudden, so unexpected, that he almost couldn't hide his reaction.

"Abraham said you wanted to ask me some questions?"

Mike realized that Kyle was going to let him move

at his own pace. Maybe they had once been good friends. This was difficult, but he knew the best way was to dive straight in. "Tell me about my relationship with Marcelle Ricco."

Kyle held his steady gaze. "That's one thing I always liked about you, Duke. No beating around the bush. You don't remember anything?"

"Nothing. I don't even know what she looked like."

"That's too bad. She was a beautiful woman. I'd say she liked you a lot."

Mike felt his hopes sink. So he had known this woman. "Go on," he said.

"Marcelle did a lot of business with you. She had expensive tastes and you gave her a good price on the things she wanted imported. It was a lucrative business deal for both of you." He motioned to the bartender. "To be honest, I never knew how deep your friendship with her went. There were times I thought you might have something going with her, but then there was always Liza. I would have said you were completely devoted to Liza." He shrugged. "But then—"

"Then what?" Mike was annoyed when the bartender came over and interrupted, but he ordered a soft drink and waited.

"Well, just before you disappeared and Marcelle turned up dead, the two of you had a falling out. She'd ordered some Chinese panels from you. When they were delivered to her home, she wanted you to come and take a look at them. You sent Regis, but she wouldn't let him in. She said she wanted only you."

"Was it unusual for her to ask that of me?"

Kyle gave him a long look. "If it had been any other customer, you would have sent Regis and been done with it. Instead, you were in such a hurry to go over there that it made me wonder.''

"And I went. What happened?"

"You never came back. And her body was found the next morning, stabbed three times.''

"Do you know if I made it to her home?"

Kyle shook his head. "When you didn't turn up at the office, I waited until about eight o'clock. We had an order from Tunisia tied up in a border conflict and a lot of capital was at stake. You were supposed to make some phone calls, get the ball rolling through channels to get that order on the move. When you hadn't returned by nine, I drove over to Marcelle's. I was curious. Something wasn't right, but I couldn't put my finger on it. I had talked to Marcelle, and she was just so…adamant about your coming personally. It sounded fishy to me.''

Mike clenched his hand under the table. "What did she tell you? Was I still there?"

Kyle gave him another long, considering look. "I don't know. No one ever came to the door. Your vehicle wasn't there. I rang the bell half a dozen times and finally gave it up and went home for the night. As I recall, I had a late date.''

Mike digested the information. His hope that Kyle LaRue could give him something solid was rapidly dwindling. "Was I being set up?"

"That's a real possibility. But the question is by whom. And why? Marcelle bought a lot of things from you, but she benefited, too.''

"What do you mean?"

"I always assumed you provided her with names of your international customers for her guest lists.''

Mike was at a loss. "I don't know." It didn't seem

like something he would do, but then he'd been a very different man.

"Have you seen a doctor about your amnesia? Five years is a long time. Any chance you'll get your memory back?"

Mike nodded. "I went to a couple of specialists. They tried a few things to stimulate my memory. Nothing worked."

"And you don't remember anything? Nothing about the business or how much you loved finding beautiful things and placing them in homes? Nothing about the business at all?"

"Nothing," Mike said, feeling the emptiness that was his past engulf him.

"If the cops find out you're back in town, they'll try to arrest you. Be careful, man."

"Is there anyone who might know exactly where I went after I left the office?"

"Liza Hawkins." Kyle's eyebrows rose. "Have you seen Liza?"

"In a manner of speaking."

"She's become very hot these days. Her name is being bandied about by all the art critics."

"I know."

"Be careful, Duke. If you don't figure this out, you're going to pay the price for Marcelle's murder. If there's anything I can do to help..."

"Thanks, Kyle."

"I heard Liza's dating some detective." He shook his head. "This is too much." He started to say something else, then stood up.

"What?" Mike asked, also rising.

"Be careful, Duke. You were always straight with me. When the cops came to question me about your relationship with Marcelle, the implications they made were pretty clear.''

"It would have to be blackmail, right?''

"That's right. But there was something else that troubled me. Watch out for that artist. She may know more than she's let on. Right before you left the office, you got a call from her. I know because I was using the computer on your desk to track a shipment from Venice. I was still in the office when you said you'd meet her. But she told the cops she didn't talk to you that day. She lied.''

## Chapter Eight

Moonlight glazed the bronze statue of Andrew Jackson on his horse, and Liza studied the effects on the cold metal. The silvery lighting didn't bring the statue to life, but etched it in ice. Moonlight was better served by pen and ink than watercolor, she decided, and her left hand twitched as she imagined sketching the statue. It had been years since she'd considered using her pen on a subject other than Duke Masonne.

Duke! She checked her watch. It was almost midnight. Duke had always been punctual. On the button. She'd arrived fifteen minutes early in a deliberate effort to give herself a little time to calm her nerves.

The showing of her artwork had gone as smoothly as if it had been choreographed. The only rough spot was when the newspaper critic had asked her about her abrupt departure from the LaTique Gallery showing.

For a moment, Liza had been flustered—especially when Anita Blevins had pointed out that Liza had stood her up for lunch. Profuse apologies had taken the edge off Anita's anger, but Liza knew she'd done severe damage to her relationship with the art critic. Pascal would be furious if he heard about it. Liza had attempted to patch things up with another interview appointment—one she had to make tomorrow.

But that was insignificant, really, in light of the fact that Duke was alive and well. Or at least physically well. He'd lost his memory. It was something you'd expect in a television drama, not real life, but it had happened to a man with keen intelligence. It didn't matter, though. What mattered was that he was alive and that in another minute he'd be standing in front of her.

She'd deliberately chosen midnight at Jackson Square. When she and Duke had begun to see each other, they'd taken it slowly. The attraction between them had been so instantaneous, the chemistry so sizzling, that both had stepped back from it. They'd been dating for several weeks when they'd found themselves in the park Square after a cocktail party at Bella Luna.

In the silvery moonlight, Liza had given in to the breathless desire to kiss Duke. That first kiss had told them both that whatever the future held, the present was inevitable. The passion they'd both fought so long and hard to control flamed over them. Hand in hand, they'd walked to her apartment and made love. Liza had known then that Duke was the only man she'd ever truly love. That moment in the square had been the beginning of something rare and wonderful for Liza. Deep in her heart, she hoped the setting would evoke a memory for Duke.

Another wave of doubt set in, and Liza toyed with the lapis stone that hung between her breasts on the unusual silver chain.

Was it possible that she was actually meeting the

man she'd loved for so long? Or was this another de-lusion, a worsening of her mental state?

"Meow." The cat rubbed against her legs, and she bent down and scooped him into her arms.

"I hope we're doing the right thing." She couldn't deny she was apprehensive.

Familiar hopped to the ground and darted toward the northwest entrance of the park where St. Louis Cathedral stood stark and eerie. "Me-ow!" he de-manded.

"Not on your life. I'm not going sight-seeing," Liza said. The cat was determined to get her up and following him, but she wasn't leaving her place for love nor money. It was time—the church bell began to toll the hour of midnight. Liza felt the ring of the old bell all the way to her heart.

"Meow!" Familiar was back at her leg, his sharp claws digging into her bare skin.

"Stop it," she said to the cat. "I'm not leaving here."

"Liza."

The name seemed to come out of the darkness, and Liza and the cat both turned to the dark silhouette that began to move out of the shadow of an oak tree and toward them.

"Duke." Liza rose to her feet. Her heart was pounding and she felt as if she might lose her balance.

"I thought you might not come," he said.

"I knew you would," she replied, finding that it was true. As long as Duke was flesh and blood, she knew he'd show up. In the three years they'd been together, he'd never let her down. Except for that last night, when he'd vanished without a trace.

The lights of the park remained behind him, and

Duke's features were cast in shadow. Liza was suddenly consumed with a need to see him more clearly. Stepping forward, she shifted so that the light fell on his face.

"I thought I'd never see you again," she whispered, reaching out to touch his jaw. "Five years, Duke. Five years of wondering."

His dark eyes didn't waver. "I always wondered about my past, but I was lucky, I suppose. I had work. Physical work. And I found people who grew to care about me. But then, you've done well for yourself, too."

Unexpectedly, Liza felt a sob rise in her throat. They were talking to each other as if they'd been friends a long, long time ago—a passion now only in the past. "Oh, Duke."

Something in her voice must have touched him, as his cool expression gave way to sudden pain. "I'd give anything to remember," he admitted. "Whatever I shared with you, it must have been spectacular."

Liza stepped closer, all thoughts of safety or caution evaporating, pushed aside by her feelings for the man who stood before her. She didn't wait for him to kiss her. She stood on tiptoe and brushed her lips softly against his. "I've dreamed of this moment for five years," she said, her arms going around his neck.

The feel of his hard body against her brought back a wave of memories that swept over her. She felt her body begin to tremble and knew there was no stopping it. She'd spent too many lonely nights dreaming of this moment. Maybe she was insane. Maybe she was making the biggest mistake of her life, but she didn't care.

For a moment, Duke merely accepted her kiss, but

then his arms closed around her and Liza gave herself to the pleasure of his mouth on hers.

If at first his kiss was tentative, it took only seconds for his passion to ignite. His mouth became more demanding, releasing a flood of memories in her.

The soft darkness of the night cloaking them, Liza felt Duke's hands grasp her waist. Her heart was pounding, and beneath his cotton shirt, she could feel his answering heartbeat.

When his lips moved down to her neck, she arched her back, giving him access to the tender flesh. She'd never wanted him more.

"Come back with me to my place," she urged, the heat of her passion making her voice low and throaty.

That simple request brought him up short. He eased her away from him so that he could look into her eyes. His own were glazed with desire. "I know you," he said, his voice hoarse. "When you're in my arms, I feel as if I've known you...but I don't really remember."

Liza felt a twist of pain. "Maybe you don't have to remember, Duke. I remember well enough for both of us."

"The past is unavoidable. I can't pretend that it isn't. For a lot of reasons."

She reached up and touched his lips with a finger. "Let me help you find it," she said. "Together, we can find out the truth. I know we can."

"Are you sure? There are things that you don't know—"

She cut him off. "I've never been more sure."

"All right." He caught her hand in his and kissed her fingertips. Together, they walked out of the park and the few short blocks to her building.

MIKE STEPPED INTO the gallery where three dozen of Liza's pictures were hanging. He knew them all by heart. He'd examined them again and again from the sidewalk. It seemed the scenes were strangely familiar and yet he couldn't place them in his past. He had little time to think about them as Liza opened the elevator door and took them to the third floor.

She was watching him as he stepped out of the elevator, and he knew she was looking for some hint of recognition on his face. With the doubts that he had about her and about himself, he had no business being with her in this way. But he found that he couldn't deny himself. The feel of her was like the most potent of drugs. Her velvety skin demanded his touch. He wanted nothing more than to kiss her lips, to drown his doubts and worries in the passion she aroused in him.

The tiny portion of his brain that warned of caution was overwhelmed by his desire for this woman. His need for her. He could only compare it to a feeling of desperate hunger, as if he were starving. Liza was the only sustenance that would satisfy that hunger. Not just any woman, but Liza. Only Liza. He heard the soft groan that escaped him as he pulled her into his arms again.

Then there was no time for thoughts of any kind. They tugged at each other's clothes. He had the zipper of her silky dress running smoothly down her back. With both hands, he pushed it from her shoulders, sliding it down her hips. The midnight-blue bra was next, then the lacy scrap of panties, the satiny blue a vivid contrast to her pale skin.

Her hands were busy at his belt buckle, and with her help he was out of his clothes in no time.

Taking his hand, she led him to the bedroom. For a split second, he felt as if he knew where he was. The sheer curtains billowing in the soft April breeze seemed to echo a memory. But he had no time to explore the past—the present was too all-consuming.

As his hands began to move down Liza's body, he had the strangest sensation. He knew her—knew the flesh that responded to his slightest touch. In the darkness, with the scent of honeysuckle on the breeze, he had a flash of another place, another time. There was a patchwork quilt on the bed, and Liza upon it. She was laughing up at him, her golden curls spread about her like sunshine in silk. Those were the only details, but he was filled with a sense of happiness.

"Liza," he said, knowing that he was deeply connected with the woman he placed gently on the bed. "I remember," he said softly, amazed at the power of it.

"I do, too," she answered, rising up to kiss him, drawing him close to her and to a pleasure so intense that neither remembering nor thinking was possible.

LIZA TRACED DUKE'S handsome profile with her fingertips as he slept. He was sound asleep, the lines of worry and concern erased from his features. The pleasure of watching him was almost too much to bear. She felt tears sting her eyes and blinked them away. He might not remember his past, but he remembered how to make love to her. He knew exactly how to touch her. The chemistry between them had been as intense as ever. They were perfectly in sync with one another on a physical level. Whatever else had changed, that had not.

"I love you," she whispered. "There's a good chance that I'm crazy, but I still love you."

It was three in the morning, but Liza knew she wouldn't sleep. Her heart was too full. Duke was back in her life. In her bed. Had she not known better, she could almost forget the past five years. But when the morning came, the past would have to be dealt with.

And that past opened the door on a lot of ugly possibilities. Duke was a suspect in a murder. He had a past he hadn't shared completely with her. Marcelle Ricco had become, for her, a woman of glamour and mystery. Duke had known her both professionally and personally. As she traced her fingertip ever so lightly along the edge of his sensuous mouth, she wondered about his amnesia. Pascal and Trent had made it clear they thought his loss of memory was all too convenient. Was it? If not deliberate, was it some mental trick he was playing on himself so that he didn't have to confront an ugly truth?

A scuttling sound outside the bedroom window sent a sharp jab of fear up her spine. Only the night before, her place had been broken into, no matter what the police said. And something—or someone—was now outside on her balcony.

The temptation to wake Duke was almost irresistible, but her fear intensified as her complete trust of the man asleep beside her wavered. He'd reappeared in her life, a phantom from the past. Since she'd begun to catch glimpses of him, her life had turned upside down.

Her home had been violated, a painting destroyed, and the antique pen left for her to find sticking in the throat of her drawing of Duke.

The soft sound of something outside the window

came again. Liza eased off the bed, wondering what she should do. Calling the police was out of the question. Duke was wanted by them. Indecision made her want to pace, but she held steady and listened.

The sheer curtains undulated on the soft breeze that only a moment before had seemed so wonderful. Now there was the hint of something sinister in their movements. It was almost as if somebody was creeping beneath them.

The soft sound came again—one of her ceramic pots scraping on the wooden floor of the balcony.

Duke remained solidly asleep, and Liza almost went to him. Instead, she walked to the window. It was foolish to let a tiny noise terrify her. The sensible thing was to look outside and see what was on her balcony. Probably a pigeon. She slipped into an old T-shirt and a pair of jeans.

Just as she pushed the curtains aside, something leaped from the open window into the room. Her scream lodged in her throat, feeling as if it would tear the flesh. To her shock, she recognized the intruder— Familiar! Her relief was so sweet that she grabbed the cat, clutching him under her chin.

"How did you get up to the third floor?" she asked him, kissing his black fur. "You scared ten years off my life."

Instead of purring, the cat gave a low growl. He spit at the window, wiggling free of Liza's embrace.

"What?" she said, moving after him toward the window.

Then she heard it—the sound of leather on metal. Someone really was outside. This wasn't the soft sound she'd heard earlier. This was a man, or possibly men. And they were coming up the fire escape.

She stepped through the gauzy curtains, then forced herself to the balcony and looked down. The man climbing up the fire escape was stealthy, his movements quick and guarded. In the bright moonlight, she caught a glimpse of the gun he held in his right hand, a menacing blue-black weapon.

"Duke!" Liza rushed to the bed. "Duke, there's someone outside."

He woke instantly and was on his feet, already half-dressed. "Who is it?"

"I don't know," Liza said, her voice shaking with fear. "What are we going—"

She didn't have time to finish. Someone vaulted through the window, tumbling as he entered the room. Before Liza could even utter a sound, Duke was on him, fists flailing. The gun skittered across the floor, and Liza watched, petrified, as the black cat snagged it with a paw and dragged it under the sofa, safely out of the reach of both men.

"Duke," Liza cried when he took a slug to the jaw.

He didn't answer, except to return the favor to the intruder.

"I'm calling the police," Liza said. It didn't matter that Duke might get in trouble. If she didn't do something, he might get killed.

She snapped on the light just as Duke caught the man with a solid right to the jaw. The intruder dropped to the floor, out cold. Liza looked down and saw that the intruder was none other than Trent Maxwell. He'd been knocked senseless, but he stirred slightly on the floor.

"Trent!" Instinctively, she bent over him and felt for a pulse.

"Does your boyfriend always use the fire escape to

make his early-morning entrances?'' Duke asked as he wiped blood from the corner of his mouth.

''He isn't...'' But Liza didn't finish. In a way, Trent was her boyfriend. Though they hadn't been intimate, they'd been seeing each other. She called it a friendship, but she was aware that Trent wanted more.

''Spare me,'' Duke said, pulling on his cowboy boots. ''Next time you invite your current boyfriend over, maybe you shouldn't drag up someone from your past.''

Liza was stunned at his seemingly irrational anger. ''What's wrong with you?''

''Forgive me if I'm not real happy about being set up.'' Duke had all of his clothes back on. He went to the door, his hand on the knob. ''I trusted you, Liza. When did you call the cops? While I was asleep?''

''What are you accusing me of?'' Her fear quickly turned to anger at his unfair assumptions.

Duke let his gaze linger on her hand, still at Trent's neck. ''I don't know who I am—or who you are. I can't trust myself, much less you. This is the man who's already tried to shoot me. The man you've been seeing. Forgive my cynicism, but the circumstances seem a little convenient.''

''I didn't call anyone.'' Liza felt like a fool for even defending herself.

''Then you have the strangest social life of anyone I know. You'll understand if I don't really want to participate in it.''

''Duke..'' Liza didn't finish. He'd closed the door and was gone.

She turned to the man on the floor who was moaning. She knew she should feel remorse at the fact that he had been knocked unconscious, but she felt only anger.

She knelt beside him, putting a hand on his forehead. "Take it easy, Trent," she said.

He opened his eyes. "Where's Masonne?"

"He's gone," she said, feeling another wave of anger. Trent had broken into her home knowing that the man with her was Duke.

"Damn!" He raised himself up on an elbow, shook his head and sat up. "My gun."

She motioned to the sofa where Familiar had knocked it. "Under there." After Trent retrieved it, she sat down on the side of the bed, elbows on her knees. "Whatever possessed you to break in here like that?"

"You might not want to believe it, Liza, but Duke Masonne is a wanted man. He's a suspect in a murder case. Marcelle Ricco's murder has been reopened. There's a warrant being issued right now for Masonne's arrest. I was trying to protect you." He took in her tousled hair and the rumpled bed. "I was trying to protect myself, too. Looks like I'm too late."

Trying to control her anger at Trent's actions, Liza focused on fact. "A warrant? For Duke? Did you have anything to do with that?"

Trent looked away from her. "I did, and I don't regret it. After all this time, you're still in love with that man. He abandoned you and yet you still can't see him for what he is."

"He doesn't remember, Trent."

"I've been told that amnesia is a malady of convenience."

"That's not fair."

"What isn't fair is that you let that man into your home knowing he might have killed a woman."

"Might." She stood up. "That's the important word. Might have killed. And I don't believe it. Duke might not remember the past, but I do. I know who he is. I was going to marry him—because he was a man worthy of my love. I can't forget that just because he has an illness. Yes, I'm concerned about the past and what happened, but I have to believe in Duke. You say he's wanted for murder—there's no evidence that he did anything. He was never charged with anything. Accusations are easy to make and hard to prove."

"We have enough evidence now to issue a warrant." Trent rose to his feet, his hand on the armoire for support. "I care what happens to you. That's why I came in here alone, to spare you embarrassment. And since I didn't think Masonne would stick around to answer questions if I knocked on the front door."

Liza shook her head. "You just wanted to capture Duke and charge him."

Trent's jaw was clenched tight. "That's true. I do. But if he's innocent, the best thing he could do would be to work with me. You might tell him that. As long as he doesn't turn himself in, then we have to view him as a prime suspect."

Liza walked out of the bedroom and into the kitchen. "I won't get a chance to tell him a damn thing, thanks to you. He thinks I called the cops on him. How did you know he was here?"

"We've had someone tailing you for a couple of weeks now. We saw you in Jackson Square. Remember, you asked for protection when you were afraid that someone was following you."

Realization struck Liza hard and fast. Familiar had tried to warn her of something in the square. He'd done all he could to get her attention and she'd ignored him. Trent's eleventh-hour appearance also explained how he'd come to be on the levee the night he'd shot at Duke. He'd been tailing her then, too. As angry as she was at him, she also understood. He was doing his best to protect her even though it was the one thing she didn't want. Pascal had asked for protection for her—and she hadn't actually fought against it.

Trent followed her into the kitchen. "I know you're upset with me now, but when you have time to think this through, you'll thank me."

Liza bit back her angry reply. "I think you should go." She was bone weary, suddenly so tired she didn't think she could even shuffle back to bed. If she could only get some sleep, things might seem better in the morning. The one thing she absolutely didn't want to do was think about Duke and his ugly accusations.

"Call Pascal," Trent said.

"No. I don't want him here and I don't want to disturb him."

"I don't like leaving you alone."

Liza didn't look at Trent. She couldn't. For the first time in five years, she hadn't been alone. She'd been with the man she loved more than life itself. And then Trent had burst through the window. Now she was more alone than ever.

"Please, Trent, just leave."

"I'll call you tomorrow."

She nodded without answering. Tomorrow seemed like an eternity away.

"Liza, we've turned up more evidence that implicates this man in Marcelle Ricco's murder."

Liza didn't want to hear it. She didn't want to hear anything except silence. She kept her eyes averted, hoping he would leave.

"We found a list of Masonne's top clients. It was hidden in her study, and was missed during the initial investigation. Beside the list of names was a list of figures. There were matching amounts paid into her checking account. She was blackmailing those men."

"I don't see the connection." She didn't want to defend Duke, but she couldn't help herself.

"There were equal payments made into his business account on the same day. It would appear that he and Marcelle were in on the blackmail scheme together. He probably killed her when she got greedy and tried to turn the tables on him."

# Chapter Nine

The soft, midmorning light gave the elegant old home the look of an aging lady, but one that held the secret of her age with graceful lines and gracious beauty. Though Mike didn't know much about architecture, he recognized what he liked. The turreted Gothic Victorian appealed to him. It was a far cry from the ranch houses he'd become used to, with their big timbers and roaring fireplaces. This period house had a unique, old-fashioned charm.

It was Marcelle Ricco's house, the former location of her famous parties and the discreet escort service she ran. Mike had been staring at it for several hours— ever since the sun came up. No matter how hard he concentrated, he still couldn't remember ever having crossed the threshold.

Yet he must have. Kyle had told him so—at least once, to check on the Chinese panels. As for other reasons for visiting, there was the implication that his relationship with Marcelle had been as much personal as business. Whenever Mike looked at her picture, though, he felt nothing. Marcelle had been a beautiful woman, no doubt about it. Yet no matter how he tried, he could feel nothing for her.

And then there was Liza Hawkins, for whom he felt far too much.

From Liza's bed, he'd gone down to the docks, wandering in the night like a seaman who'd lost his ship. That was what it seemed like.

In the past five years, he'd always felt as if he were living on the fringes of another man's life. He'd been granted the right to live there, but he'd never be able to feel he really belonged. He'd always remain slightly on the outside, a stranger looking in. In bed with Liza, he truly felt as if he'd found his home.

What a joke. She'd called her boyfriend cop on him the minute he was asleep.

*But she could have set him up in the park.*

He closed his eyes as he argued with himself. None of it made sense to him. Nothing that he'd learned. At the heart of his problem was Liza Hawkins. His feelings for her were in direct contradiction to what his brain told him. The past and present had overlapped in her.

The only thing he could do was concentrate on Marcelle Ricco. She was the key that would unlock his past. When he discovered what had happened to her, he'd know who'd beaten him and robbed him of his identity. Then someone was going to pay.

Marcelle's house looked empty, but Mike questioned that observation. He'd been in New Orleans only a short time, but it was long enough to determine that real estate was at a premium, especially in such an elite neighborhood.

Marcelle had been wealthy. Whatever her trade, she'd been successful at it. Abraham had told him Marcelle often spent better than a hundred thousand dollars a year buying furnishings and artwork from

Masonne International. She had ample funds and paid in cash—according to Kyle LaRue.

Mike had tried to reconstruct the day of his disappearance. He'd talked to Abraham and Kyle. The best that he'd been able to piece together was that he'd been at the office until closing time when Marcelle had phoned, begging him to come and take a look at her new purchases. She wanted to have them ready for one of her soirees. According to Kyle, Marcelle had insisted that she wanted to see Duke himself.

Duke had headed over to her house, saying he would return to make some phone calls to clear up a problem with an order from Tunisia. He'd never returned to the office—had, in fact, disappeared without a trace.

From the newspaper accounts, Mike knew that Marcelle's body had been discovered by one of her girlfriends. Mike, who'd combed the back issues of the newspaper in the library, had decided the young woman had probably worked for Marcelle. She'd been pretty enough in the photos. Her name was Lisbeth Dendrich. Mike had checked the phone book—no listing. He'd searched back issues of the newspaper for any inkling of where she might have gone. Frustrated by the lack of information, he'd concluded that she was either married or long gone from New Orleans.

So now all he had to go on was the house. Marcelle had been murdered in her bedroom. Mike glanced up and down the street before he climbed the wrought-iron fence and slipped across the yard.

It was foolishness to think such a lovely house would remain empty. Still, he had no other leads to follow. This, at least, might offer a clue. He could only hope that the house was as vacant as it looked.

He went to the back and checked the kitchen window where the curtains had been left slightly apart. There were furnishings in the kitchen, but everything looked so untouched. There was an eerie emptiness about the place.

Pushing on the back door, he was surprised when it swung open without a complaint. He walked into the kitchen and stopped. Something wasn't right. The house felt empty, yet there were dirty dishes in the sink. Dirty champagne glasses, to be more exact. More than a dozen of them. He opened the refrigerator and saw four bottles of Asti Spumante. Nothing else.

At the sound of someone clearing her throat, he turned to find himself face-to-face with a woman who'd once been beautiful. Now she looked merely worn.

"Hello, Duke," she said. "I heard you were in town. I wondered how long it would take for you to find me."

LIZA'S HAND CLUTCHED her napkin, but she forced a smile as Anita Blevins finished her question. The interview had turned into a disaster. Anita had been primed to draw blood, and after a few initial questions about painting, she'd turned to tabloid questions about Duke Masonne.

"I don't believe Duke killed anyone," Liza said as calmly as she could. All around her, the restaurant echoed with laughter and the sound of cutlery on china. It was a place she normally loved. Now, though, she only wanted to escape. Anita Blevins was extracting more than her pound of flesh for one missed interview.

"You were deeply in love with him, I suppose. I'd

just come to New Orleans right before this happened. In fact, I was scheduled to go to Marcelle Ricco's home to view her art collection. I understand your Duke was…invaluable in helping her put together her pieces.''

''Duke sold artwork to people all over the world.''

Anita smiled. ''My, my, you still protect him after all these years when he didn't even bother to give you a call. He didn't even have the decency to be dead.''

Anita's comment dropped like a stone in a well, splashing loudly and echoing. ''How do you know Duke isn't dead?''

Anita's eyebrows arched. ''It's my job to know such things. And I'm very, very good at my job.''

Liza knew she had to deflect Anita's interest in Duke and her personal life. For Duke's sake as well as her own. She was dying to know where Anita had gotten her information, but asking would only keep the conversation on Duke. ''The past is just that—the past. I thought you wanted to talk about my paintings. About the future.''

''Of course, but you have to admit, Liza, that your paintings are filled with the past. There's a certain quality to them that brings back childhood. A playfulness of light in some of the more joyful ones and a sense of loss in others. What do you have to say about that?''

''Art is about joy and life. I paint what I feel.''

''But you haven't been painting watercolors lately. I hear you're interested in acrylics—a certain realism.''

Liza didn't answer. Her work was changing. But how had Anita Blevins learned this detail?

"Do you think Duke Masonne's return will affect your painting?" Anita pressed.

"Life and art aren't disconnected. Everything in life influences my work." Liza looked down at her plate. The grilled Portobello mushrooms were one of her favorite dishes. Now she couldn't swallow a bite.

"Is something wrong with your lunch?" Anita asked.

"No," Liza said. "I had a late breakfast. I'm not hungry."

"I hope my questions haven't upset you."

Liza forced a smile. "Of course not. I had a late night with the gallery opening. It was so wonderful I had trouble sleeping when I got home. Now I'm paying the price for my Cinderella night." Pascal would be delighted with that turn of phrase.

"What about the antique pen you discovered in your apartment? Any idea who might be stalking you? This story just gets better and better."

"How did you know about that?" Liza realized she was giving herself away, but she couldn't hide her dismay that Anita had learned so much about her life. It was a private matter, intensely personal.

"I work for a newspaper, Liza. We monitor police calls. I probably know more about the investigation than you do." She ate a bite of her tenderloin. "Is it true the pen was used to sketch the portraits of Louis XIV?"

Liza slowly laid her napkin on the table. "Yes, that's all true."

"Do you think Duke was responsible for returning the pen?"

Pushing back her chair, Liza had to force herself to remain seated. "I seriously doubt it. The police believe the pen was stuck somewhere in my desk. That seems to be a more likely explanation. Duke isn't the kind of person who sneaks around planting things in people's homes.''

''Or the kind to kill?''

''Or the kind to kill,'' she answered. She was ready to go, but to turn tail and run would create more trouble. Anita would take it as a sign of defeat and really move in for the kill.

''You look rather delicate,'' Anita pointed out. ''I hope I haven't unduly upset you. This piece will definitely up the circulation. Love, murder, mystery, a man from the past.'' She rubbed her arms. ''It sends chills all over me.''

The blur of black was so fast that Liza almost didn't recognize the cat. She had left him in her apartment. Now he was suddenly in the middle of one of New Orleans's most exclusive restaurants. Even better, he was stealing Anita Blevins's hunk of tenderloin.

Anita's scream echoed off the walls, halting all conversation in the restaurant.

Oblivious, Familiar lifted the hunk of meat in his mouth and stared directly into the critic's eyes. Around the meat he gave a low growl.

''Get this beast off the table!'' Anita cried, knocking her glass of red wine into her lap in her frantic attempts to get up. ''Waiter! *Garçon!* Someone, help me!''

''Oh, Anita, are you afraid of a cat?'' Liza asked with satisfaction.

''Get him!'' Anita roared.

Liza dropped cash on the table to cover the meal and tip, then scooped Familiar into her arms. ''I'll take care of him.'' Without another word, she carried the cat, tenderloin still in his mouth, out of the restaurant.

Once they were on the sidewalk, Familiar dropped the meat and began to purr.

''I don't know how you came to be so smart,'' Liza said, nuzzling the cat's neck as he purred, ''but you are the best thing that's happened to me in years. Thanks.''

''Meow,'' Familiar said, his motor turning up to high gear.

*METHINKS IT'S HIGH TIME someone put that hussy Anita Blevins in her rightful place—under the table. How dare she talk to Liza in such a fashion?*

*What concerns me is that this whole "murder" investigation has more leaks in it than the White House. I don't doubt Poison Pen Blevins heard all the details of the pen incident over a police scanner, but what I want to know is why Trent Maxwell allowed his men to talk freely over an airway that he must have known was monitored by the newspapers. It would seem that someone who truly cared for Liza would want to protect her from humiliation and embarrassment.*

*I've put a lot of thought into what's been going on. The simplest thing would be for Mike/Duke to regain his memory. If he did wake up a killer, I think he'd split. Not exactly the solution that ends in justice, but it would spare Liza—and Liza is my ultimate responsibility.*

*I did a little supersleuthing around Jackson Square this morning while Liza was getting dressed. I'm fascinated by the tourists who plop down in front of a weirdo in a turban and bad eye shadow and fork over twenty bucks for a glimpse of the future. Some of these* so-called psychics are obviously phonies! They couldn't even get a bit part in a John Waters movie, they're so bad.

But I did notice one little braided Swiss Miss. Being a feline with supersensitive powers, I can't claim that I could see this woman's aura, but I can say that there was a sense of peace about her. And because I'm black and cunning, I headed under an azalea bush and eavesdropped a bit on her conversation with a friend.

Her name is Betta, and she's from the land of watches, Alps and Heidi. She also speaks seven languages and most recently worked in a hospice where she helped suffering humanoids move on to the next plane. In other words, she isn't your average con artist.

In her conversation, she mentioned that she was interested in past-life regressions. Now I don't exactly want to take Mike/Duke back to his days as Conan the Barbarian, but it would be nice to trip backward in time about five years to the fateful night of Marcelle's murder and Duke's beating.

With this ploy in mind, I have to get Liza to follow me to the square. Somehow I have to make her think that Betta might be able to help Duke. What the heck, it can't hurt to try. I know Mike/Duke said he'd gone to a couple of doctors to try to regain his memory, but even though I love Dr. Dolittle and greatly admire the work of even the less educated humanoid physicians, sometimes what's needed is something a bit more...shall we say, spiritual?

Call it a hunch—and this feline is full of hunches—but I want to give this a try. It's just a matter of manipulating the bipeds into position to make it happen.

Ah, here's my chance. A leap from Liza's arms, a

*cry of pain and distress, a fake limp toward Betta's booth. Yes, both of them are bending over me to minister to my wounds. A fake swoon and I'll just rest here a moment and enjoy the attention of two lovely women. Kitty heaven.*

"SO YOU REALLY DON'T remember," the woman said, walking past Mike and going to the refrigerator. "Care for a drink?" She expertly opened the bottle, pulling the cork with a tiny *poof.* "Better than champagne," she said.

"No thanks." Mike stared at her. He recognized her, but not from the past. She was Lisbeth Dendrich. Or what remained of her. She looked like she'd aged twenty years since her photograph had been in the newspaper.

"Marcelle left me her house," she said, waving the bottle around the kitchen. "Generous of her, wasn't it?"

"Very." Mike felt as if the ground were shifting under him. Since he had no recollection of the past, he didn't know what Lisbeth's relationship with Marcelle might have been. Close, to say the least, since she'd inherited a home worth half a million.

"You're wanting to know what I know, aren't you?"

"That would be helpful."

"Why should I help you?"

Mike couldn't think of a reason. "Because I need your help," was the best he could do.

Lisbeth laughed. "That's rich. Really rich. The powerful Duke Masonne needs my help. Do you remember the last thing you said to me?"

"I don't remember you at all," Mike admitted.

She laughed. "That's good. We can have a clean slate, start all over. I had it bad for you, once. The last thing you said to me was that your heart belonged to Liza and where your heart went, your body followed."

Mike watched Lisbeth as she almost fell into a chair. She was slightly drunk. It was hardly morning and she was already tipsy. It looked as if she'd been drinking steadily for the past several years.

"The newspaper article said you found Marcelle." He had to focus the conversation.

"It was a bloody mess. That may have been the last time I was sober." Lisbeth laughed, but it wasn't with humor. "She told me it was going to happen. She said she'd pushed too hard."

"Who?" Mike asked, suddenly feeling he'd discovered something important. "Who was it she pushed?"

Lisbeth poured another glass of sparkling wine. "She never said. I told this to the cops and they said it was you. I never believed that, though. Marcelle had plans for you, but it wasn't to blackmail."

"So she *was* involved in a blackmail scheme."

"No doubt about that. I just don't know who she was putting the screws to." Lisbeth laughed and shook her head. "That was a good one, huh?"

"Do you know anything that might help me?" Mike was ready to go. Watching Lisbeth Dendrich destroy herself wasn't pleasant. The past events had taken a heavy toll on many people. He was only one of them.

"I do know that whatever Marcelle was doing, it involved art."

"Are you certain?" Mike had assumed that Marcelle's escort service was the basis of her blackmail scheme.

"Yes, it was art. I know because she made several jokes about how sex was so accepted, but…"

"But what?"

"But she said theft was still frowned upon by the general public."

"Theft." Mike spoke the word aloud, but it was for his benefit, not Lisbeth's. "May I see some of the pieces I obtained for her?"

"Sure. *Mi casa, su casa.* Follow me."

Lisbeth led the way into the parlor. Mike was struck by the portrait over the mantel. It was a painting of Marcelle Ricco, and one that did her justice. "She was a lovely woman," he said, watching Lisbeth's reaction to the painting.

"She was good to me. She didn't deserve to die." Lisbeth turned to him. "If I truly believed you'd killed her, I'd call the cops."

"Why do you believe I'm innocent?"

Lisbeth's smile was sad. "You were a straight arrow, Duke. You had a knack for making money, but you were never greedy. You gave good value. I suppose when you turned me down because of your girlfriend, it made an impression on me. I always wanted a man who felt like that about me. I just never met another one."

"Thanks for telling me that."

Lisbeth laughed, this time with a hint of humor. "No charge, old friend. Those vases on the mantel came from China." She went around the room, pointing out various pieces of art and furniture.

It took an hour to go through the house, and Lisbeth ended the tour in Marcelle's bedroom. It was a lavish suite, decorated with heavy pieces of rosewood from the Philippines.

"She had good taste," Lisbeth noted.

Mike stood in the room, trying to force a memory that refused to come. "I can't remember ever having set foot in this house," he said.

"Duke, are you sure you simply don't want to remember?"

Now it was his turn for a laugh—one of bitterness. "That's the million-dollar question, isn't it?"

## Chapter Ten

The black cat had finally gotten to his feet and was patting his paw on the fortune-teller's laptop desk. Liza bent to look closer. *Past-Life Regressions.* She looked at Familiar, who met her with his unwavering golden gaze.

"No," she said aloud.

"Meow."

"Absolutely not. Even if I thought it was a good idea, Duke wouldn't go for it. The very idea of such a thing makes him laugh."

"Me-ow!" Familiar's paw was as adamant as his meow.

"Besides, after this morning, he'll never speak to me again. I don't even have any idea how to get in touch with him."

The black cat winked one eye. Liza knew it was impossible, but he seemed to be telling her that *he* knew how to find Duke.

"Animals are often far more perceptive than humans ever want to believe," the young woman behind the table said.

Liza finally looked at her closely and was startled to be met by striking eyes that were as open and calm as a stretch of blue ocean. Honeyed-brown hair was braided into a long, thick weave that hung over her left shoulder. It was the most peculiar thing, but looking into the stranger's eyes, Liza felt a sense of peace.

"Are you interested in knowing your past, or is it just that the cat is interested?"

"It's not for me. It's for a friend." At the young woman's open grin, Liza had to laugh. "Yeah, I know. It sounds fishy, but it's true. I have a friend who can't remember anything beyond the past five years. I believe he was severely beaten."

"It sounds neurological rather than emotional."

At that blunt diagnosis, Liza was further impressed. "He's been to physicians and psychiatrists. They can't help him."

"Five years is a long time to go without remembering. Perhaps he has a reason to forget."

Unexpectedly, Liza felt the tears well in her eyes. Standing in Jackson Square, she was completely unashamed to cry in front of this stranger.

"Have a seat," the woman said, indicating a canvas chair. "My name is Betta. Perhaps if you talk for a moment, you'll feel better."

Liza had just sat down when Familiar jumped into her lap and proceeded to purr. With the cat's comforting presence, Liza found herself pouring out the entire story. Half an hour later, she was finished. Looking down at her watch, she felt a blush climb her cheeks. "I'm terribly sorry. I've taken your time. I can at least pay you for it."

"No charge," Betta said. "I don't know if I can help your friend or not, but I'm willing to try. To be falsely accused of something is a terrible thing. To be prosecuted for it is even worse, and it sounds like that could happen.'' She pulled a card from her backpack and handed it to Liza. ''This is my home address. If you can find your friend and convince him to come, meet me at my home at seven tonight.''

Liza rose. ''I don't know that I can find him. Even if I do, he's furious with me. He thinks I betrayed him.''

''We often accuse others of the crime we ourselves are guilty of. Perhaps he actually feels as if he's betrayed himself.''

Liza considered Betta's words. ''Thank you.''

''I hope you make it tonight. And take care of that cat of yours. He's extraordinary.''

''I know,'' Liza agreed before she headed back to the gallery.

MIKE HAD RETURNED to his apartment in the hope of taking a nap. He'd gotten almost no sleep the night before. After storming out of Liza's, he'd been too upset to rest. Now, though, he found that his thoughts wandered back to the woman he'd vowed to forget— again.

Her faint fragrance seemed to cling to his skin, a smell of flowers and sunshine. Whenever he turned over, his arm sought the curve of her waist. He missed her with a longing that was so deep he considered that he might be on the verge of losing his mind. He'd been with her one night—had talked with her one evening. Yet he felt as if the greater part of his heart had been cut out. The connection between them was stronger than anything he'd ever felt in his life, or what of it he could remember.

That bitter thought made him turn over in the bed.

He found himself eye-to-eye with the strange black cat.

"Familiar," he said, recalling that was the name Liza had called him. "Where'd you come from?"

"He came with me."

At the sound of Liza's voice, he bolted to his feet. He'd taken off his shirt, and as he reached for it, he was aware of her gaze on his bare chest.

"The door was unlocked," Liza added.

"I don't think it's a good thing that you're here," he said.

"Probably not, but I had to come." She was twisting her hands in front of her.

"How far behind you are the cops?"

"Don't do that, please. I didn't call them last night. They had a tail on me. I didn't know it. Maybe I should have, but I didn't. When I kept seeing you, catching glimpses of you outside windows and behind me, I thought someone was stalking me or that I was losing my mind. Trent said he'd keep an eye on me. I guess I just didn't understand what that meant or I never would have agreed to meet you. No matter what you think, I never would have deliberately put you in jeopardy."

Mike buttoned his shirt as he listened to her talk. She sounded so damn sincere. But wasn't that the way deceptive people were supposed to sound—sincere? People didn't give an insincere con artist a chance to bilk them.

"How did you find me?" he asked. A lot would depend on her answer to that question.

"The cat. I followed him."

Mike stopped buttoning and stared at Familiar.

"Traitor," he said. "I should have been suspicious when you turned up here the other day."

"He did move Trent's gun under the sofa," Liza reminded him. "He saved you from getting shot."

"So he did," Mike finally conceded. "What do you want, Liza? Maybe you should tell me and then leave."

"I have an appointment for you at seven. With someone who may be able to help you unlock the past."

Mike gave a half chuckle. "Right, and then I can pull rabbits out of my hat. I've tried all of this before, remember?"

"I think this woman may be able to help. She isn't a...medical person."

"What, she's a spiritualist?"

"A fortune-teller. Betta."

Mike wanted to laugh out loud, but the hope in Liza's eyes stopped him. He could have sworn that she was really trying to help him. And no effort at help, no matter how impractical, deserved to be sneered at.

"I know it sounds crazy," Liza continued, her gaze falling to her hands, which she laced and twisted in front of her. "I just happened across her...well, actually, Familiar led me to her. And when I was talking to her, it seemed like she really might be able to help. What could it hurt?"

Liza looked so young and innocent. So vulnerable. Mike knew the idea of a fortune-teller was ridiculous, but he also knew that he was probably going to go. It had taken effort for Liza to find him, to explain. He could at least do a small thing she asked, especially since it was all in an attempt to help him. "Nothing. I'll give it some thought."

"Have you found out anything new?"

Mike hesitated. She was standing in his bedroom wringing her hands like a teenager. His brain told him he was crazy to spend another moment with her, but his heart was giving him completely different directions. Desire for her was so strong that he knew if he didn't get her out of his bedroom, he'd have to kiss her—and much more. "How about a cup of coffee?" he asked.

"I'd love one."

The relief on her face and in her eyes made him ashamed that he'd been such an ass. He'd stormed out of her home and left her with a half-dozen ugly accusations. Yet she'd come back to him with another offer of help. Either she was setting him up big time or she cared for him a lot more than she cared for her pride.

"Chicory or plain?" he asked.

"You tell me," Liza said lightly.

"Chicory with two sugars and hot milk." He said it without thinking, but when he turned to look at her, he saw in the wide-open expression of her eyes that he had guessed correctly.

"What's my favorite breakfast?" she asked.

Mike felt his heartbeat increase. "French toast with bacon."

"And yours?"

He went to her, carefully placing his hands on her shoulders. "You." The tear that slipped down her cheek was almost more than he could bear. He brushed it away with his thumb. "I'm sorry, Liza. Last night...I panicked."

She shook her head. "I don't blame you. It looked like I'd set you up." She took a ragged breath. "Will you talk to Betta?"

"I don't think it'll help, but I'll try."

"You're already remembering things, Duke. The coffee, breakfast. We said those things every morning. It was a joke between us. You always fussed at me because I drank only coffee and wouldn't eat. Then you'd snatch a kiss and declare it the best breakfast you'd ever had—just before you rushed out the door."

"Liza, the day I disappeared, did you see me?"

"That morning. You left early. You had to check a shipment in at the docks and there was some trouble with customs. Then you had a meeting with some buyer from Baton Rouge. We were supposed to meet at nine for dinner at La Sal's. I waited for over two hours, but you never came. And I never heard from you again."

"You didn't see or hear from me that afternoon?"

She hesitated. "Normally, you called me when you left the office, but this time you didn't. It was odd, but I assumed you were too busy."

"What about a cell phone? Did I have one?"

"Of course."

"What happened to it?"

"I don't know." Liza shrugged. "I didn't think to ask."

"And my car? What about it?"

"It was a Land Rover. It disappeared, but the police found it a week later in Austin, Texas. It had been gutted and abandoned. The assumption at first was that whoever killed you had carjacked it." She looked him square in the eye. "Or that you'd sold it and left town, but I never believed that."

"My money and bank accounts, my business—what happened to them?"

"No relatives stepped forward. As only your fiancée, I had no claim on any of your property. Except as beneficiary of your life insurance policy."

Mike kept his face impassive.

"I was to use the money to pay off the gallery building, just as we discussed."

Mike let the facts sink in. He had more questions. More than ever. He just had to ask the right ones. "The rest of my estate and investments, the selling of the business—what about all of that?"

"As far as I know, there was no will. I assumed that everything was put in some kind of trust. No one ever told me, and I didn't ask. I never considered that I could. Pascal said that without a legal tie to you, I had no right to ask any questions or put forth any conditions."

"If no one pushed for a trust, then things are still in limbo." Mike felt the excitement begin to rush through him, and this time he didn't hide his reaction.

"What's so important?"

"I can get the books. Or you can. If I can find out what's in those books, I may be able to figure out what happened to Marcelle."

"What do your books have to do with her death?"

Mike found that his hands were back on Liza's shoulders, slowly moving up and down her arms, gently bringing her closer to him. And she made no objection.

"Do you remember a woman named Lisbeth Dendrich?"

"No." Liza's brown eyes were troubled. "Who is she?"

"She found Marcelle's body. I talked with her this morning, and she told me something that may prove to be helpful."

"Tell me." Liza stepped even closer.

The brown of her eyes had golden flecks that looked like a starburst. Mike could easily understand how a man could fall deeply in love with her. He forced his mind back onto business.

"Lisbeth seemed to think that Marcelle's death had something to do with her blackmailing art collectors, not people who used her escort business."

Liza's gaze narrowed. "How? That doesn't make sense. People who collect art generally can't be blackmailed because of it. In fact, most people are proud of their collections."

"Unless the paintings are stolen or forged."

Liza's eyes widened. "Of course! Someone trading in stolen artwork would be very vulnerable. You think you can figure this out from your books?" She remembered something Trent had told her. "In your accounts, there were deposits made that exactly mirrored deposits in Marcelle Ricco's accounts. To Trent, it looked as if you'd both received a payoff of some kind."

"I know this doesn't sound like much, but it's the first solid lead I've gotten into my past. All my financial records should be available through my lawyer. You can get those records for me."

"Can I?" Liza asked.

"Yes, with the proper credentials. I'm sure creditors have been paid, but the assets will be held."

Liza's grin widened. "Someone's sure to be very upset when they find out you're alive. Your business was sold. I do know that, and that someone's going to have to give your money back."

Mike hated to ask, but he had to. "I gather I was somewhat successful."

Liza nodded. "Very. If you're right and your assets have been held, then you'll be one happy camper." A puzzled expression crossed Liza's face. "I went down to the docks when they sold your building. It was horrible. I couldn't forget how proud of the building you were, how you'd worked with the architect to get it just right. And it was being sold, without your consent or knowledge. All I could do was watch as all of your beautiful things were removed."

"Liza, do you know where they took them?" He had a sudden idea, one that might prove to be his best course of action.

"To a warehouse down on Magazine Street. That's what Kyle told me."

"Do you know the exact address?"

Liza shook her head. "No, why?"

"Can you find out what it is?" Mike pressed.

"I'm sure I can."

"It has to be done discreetly." A terrible thought had begun to form in the back of Mike's mind. "Are you sure I didn't leave a will?"

"Positive. Your employees searched, the police searched. There wasn't any indication of a will."

"Don't you find it a little strange that a businessman as successful as I'm supposed to have been would be dumb enough not to have a will?"

He saw sudden understanding cross her face and knew that while he loved her dearly, he also had to accept that she had no head for business. She was an artist through and through.

"I feel like a fool," she said, pacing the kitchen. "You would never have done such a thing. You were meticulous in your business affairs. In fact, you insisted that *I* draw up a will."

"I want you to pay a visit to my lawyer tomorrow." Mike went to Liza and pulled her into his arms. "We may get a handle on this yet. There're a lot of things that aren't right about this, but the one thing that is absolutely right is the way you feel in my arms." He knew he should back off, wait to figure out the past, but he couldn't deny himself any longer.

Liza yielded in his arms, almost melting against him. "Oh, Duke, I was afraid you wouldn't believe me. After all this time waiting for you to come back, I thought you were going to walk away."

He buried his face in her hair, the clean smell of it bringing not a memory but again the sense of belonging. "I wanted to walk away. I wanted to go back to my life in North Dakota, where things were simpler. I know who I am there, and I'm respected and liked, not a suspect in a murder. But I couldn't walk away from you or the past." He kissed her neck, his own passion growing as he felt her respond.

Liza slipped from his arms, stepping toward the kitchen door that led to a small, secluded patio outside. The tinkling sound of a fountain drifted in through the open window.

"It's almost dusk," she said, her voice low. She carefully latched the kitchen door and turned to him. Just as slowly, she began to take off her clothes.

The rich light made her golden hair a halo that surrounded her shoulders and breasts. Mike watched her, almost breathless. He'd never seen anything more lovely in his life. He made no move toward her, only watching as she removed her dress and then her panties and bra.

"I don't care what happened in the past," she said. "What matters to me is the future. Tell me that you won't leave me."

"I didn't leave you the first time," Mike said. "I don't know what happened, but I can promise you that I didn't leave voluntarily."

"One more promise," Liza said, taking a few steps closer to him, her hair shifting in a breeze that first revealed and then covered her breasts. She seemed to shiver with anticipation.

Mike wanted to reach out for her, but he held back. There were things to be settled, and as much as he wanted to touch her, to let his passion consume them both, he waited. "What?"

"We'll go and see Betta tonight at seven."

He lifted an eyebrow. "Is this a negotiation?" He couldn't help but tease her.

Liza's smile was so delighted that he had to wonder why. "You don't remember, but this is a game we played a lot."

"Don't tell me. You always won."

"Always," Liza said, close enough now so that he could touch her. "Your word on it, Duke."

"You have my word. Liza, I'd promise you the moon right this minute, and you know it."

She laughed. "I do, and somehow you'd get it if you promised. Know one thing, Duke Masonne. You were always a man of your word."

"Then how about if I promise to make love to you so passionately that you'll never forget this moment."

Liza stood on tiptoe and kissed his lips softly. "Then you'd better get busy because there are a lot of competing memories in the unforgettable-lovemaking category.''

*AH, AT LAST WE GET DOWN to the dance of love. Man, it took them a while. I've never seen two creatures wanting each other so badly and yet sparring around as if they didn't know how to get the job done.*

*Thank goodness Clotilde and I don't suffer from such dysfunctional behavior. Then again, I shouldn't be so critical. Cats are, of course, the superior species. Not all of God's creations can be as smart as a cat.*

*While these two do the mattress tango, I think I'll take a stroll. Mike/Duke has given me some thoughts to ponder. I hate to say it, but I didn't even think of his estate. How I let that slip by me, I can't explain. I was so focused on the murder of Marcelle Ricco that I never thought to look at Mike/Duke as the possible source. But the old detective handbook lists sex and money as the two primary motives for murder. Revenge is third.*

*Sex I understand. Money I also understand. Man—and cat—need both of those to survive. Revenge is a purely humanoid motivation. Because we are a superior species, we cats settle our scores at the moment they need settling. Then we get on with our lives. It would never occur to a cat to lie around and ponder revenge. But then, humanoids lie around and ponder a lot of useless stuff.*

*Take television, for example. Can you think of a bigger waste of time? Oh, well, enough time spent on pointing out the inferiority of one of the most prolific species on the planet.*

*The evening light is stupendous. I'll stroll over to the square and see what kind of customers Betta is attracting. I think tonight is going to be very, very interesting.*

# Chapter Eleven

Liza wasn't certain what she expected, but Betta's apartment wasn't it. The place was almost austere, the blond wood of the tables and neatly arranged bookshelves showing a preference for Scandinavian design.

"Johan Lassfolk," Duke said softly to Liza, then lifted his eyebrows as he acknowledged his success at remembering a detail of design.

"Keep it up," Liza encouraged.

Betta was in the kitchen preparing a pot of herbal tea, and when she came back with the tray, she smiled at them. "Yes, Lassfolk is the designer. I admire his work. Very clean lines. So you know something about furniture, Duke?"

"I once did," he said. "Lassfolk's name just popped into my head. Lately, a few details have been coming back."

"That's a very good sign." Betta poured the tea.

Liza watched the young woman and again felt the sense of peace that had first drawn her to Betta. "When you work with someone, what do you do?" she asked.

"Depends." Betta looked first at Liza, then at Duke. "How open are you to help?"

"I want to remember. I don't know why I can't."

Betta nodded. "I have to be honest. When a person can't remember large chunks of the past, it's usually for one of two reasons—protection or deception."

Liza started to protest, then decided against it. She and Duke had come to this woman with no expectations, only hope. It was Betta's show. She had a right to say whatever she wanted.

"I've been told that before," Duke said in a tone that indicated he wasn't in the least put off by Betta's statement. "I've also been told that I found myself a safe place and hid out there for five years. But based on that theory, I must be ready to find the truth or I would have stayed in North Dakota."

Betta's smile was delighted. "Very sound reasoning. Now if you don't object, I'd like to try some hypnosis. I won't make you walk like a duck or do anything else ridiculous. Liza will make sure of that—and of course, Familiar." She gave the black cat who hopped onto the chair beside her a few pats.

"We haven't discussed your fee," Duke said.

"For this, I don't charge. This isn't a question about your future love life or the stock market. This is something that intrigues me. I'll help if I can."

"Thank you," Duke and Liza said in unison.

Liza put her hand on Duke's knee, feeling more than a little apprehensive about what she'd set in motion. "Don't go too far back," she said. "I don't want to lose you to the past now that I've gotten you back."

Betta held up a small, lighted box with multicolored beads that floated in a clear fluid. "Watch the beads, Duke," she said softly. "Just keep all your attention focused on them and listen to the sound of my voice. You are relaxing. Feel it in your body, beginning with your toes. Wiggle your toes and allow all tension to leave.'' She continued up his body, naming each part.

Liza saw Duke visibly begin to relax, his body softening from the rigid posture that had always marked his bearing. She was fascinated that he seemed to fall under Betta's direction so quickly, yet she wasn't affected at all. When Betta gave her a nod, Liza nodded in agreement. Duke seemed more relaxed than she'd ever seen him.

''Now that you're relaxed, I want you to think about the past,'' Betta said. ''The year is 1997 and it's winter. What are you doing?''

''Little Sue didn't come in with the herd. I have to find her. There's not enough grazing left up in the leeward pasture.''

Liza watched Duke's face intently. His expression had shifted from relaxed to concerned and worried. His eyes, though shut, were squinting, as if he faced a bitter wind.

Betta led him through several more exercises involving his life at the ranch, experiencing different seasons and events. In each, Duke was lucid, clear, giving exact details.

''Memory is like a puzzle,'' Betta said, looking at Liza. ''In working with people who are dying, I learned that humans—and animals—'' she gave Familiar a knowing look ''—often have access to great detail when they prepare to die. It's comforting to know that we can visit treasured moments that we thought we'd forgotten before our spirits move on.''

''I hope that's true,'' Liza said.

''It is.'' Betta's voice was assured. ''It's a great gift. Duke has shut down a major portion of his past. Perhaps we can find an entrance to it, perhaps not. It may take several attempts. Is there anything that might work as a point of entry, some object? I should have thought to tell you to bring something from the past.''

Liza instantly removed the necklace with the lapis pendant. ''I've been wearing this, but Duke hasn't noticed. He gave it to me to seal our engagement. It was his grandmother's. She was an artist and she made it.''

Betta took the necklace and examined it. ''Beautiful.'' She took Duke's hand and placed the piece of jewelry in it. ''We want to go further back in time,'' she said. ''Back to childhood. There is a lovely woman wearing this necklace. Look at it.''

Duke opened his eyes and studied the necklace.

''Can you see her, Duke? She's your grandmother. She made this necklace, which was eventually given to you. It's very special to you.''

''Nanna,'' Duke said, smiling with the open warmth of a young boy. ''Nanna, it's beautiful. Did you make it?''

Liza felt chills race over her body. Duke had not physically changed, yet she could clearly see the boy that he'd once been. And his voice was lighter, filled with such innocence.

''Where are you?'' Betta prompted.

''In the garden. Nanna and I are picking roses for the table. We're having lasagna, my favorite.''

''Are you happy?''

''Yes,'' Duke said, a child's delight clearly evident. ''Nanna said when I'm grown, she'll give the necklace to me for my bride.''

Liza's impulse was to go to Duke, to touch him and protect him. How tragic that all these wonderful memories had been beyond his reach. But she sat perfectly still, afraid that any movement would destroy the trip to the past. This was more progress than anyone else had ever made with him.

"What a lovely gesture," Betta said. "Now let's go forward in time. It's 1994. You're a grown man."

At her words, his posture straightened, his shoulders moving back, his head lifting. Gone was the child.

"You're with Liza. Do you remember Liza?"

"My God, she's beautiful."

Betta smiled at Liza. "Your love is very special. It's the bond I hope that will bring back Duke's memory." She turned to Duke. "Where are you?" she asked him.

"Liza is painting. We're in her studio, and I'm standing in the doorway watching her. Her work is incredible, but it can't compare with who she is."

Liza had never known that another's unprotected words could bring such joy—and such intense pain. Five years had slipped away from them. To know that Duke loved her as much as she did him—it was almost unbearable to think of all that time lost.

"Very good, Duke. Now we're going to go forward in time again. The year is 1995. You're driving in New Orleans, heading for the home of Marcelle Ricco. Do you know the house?"

"Yes, 1214 Emmanuel Street. The house is lovely. Marcelle has exquisite taste. There's been a problem with some things she ordered from China, some panels. I know she needs to have them ready in time for a party she's having."

Knuckles white, Liza gripped the arms of her chair. This wasn't what she expected. Somehow she'd believed that Duke's relationship with Marcelle Ricco was strictly professional. But he seemed to know all about her parties. Her stomach hurt with tension.

"Are you at Marcelle's house yet?" Betta encouraged him, using all the details that Liza had given her earlier in the afternoon.

"Yes, pulling into the driveway. That's strange. The back door is open."

Betta leaned forward. "Are you inside?"

"In the kitchen. I'm calling for Marcelle, but she doesn't answer me. Kita, the maid, doesn't answer, either. There's no one here, but the door is open. Nothing is disturbed in the house, but Marcelle is always careful. She's afraid of being robbed."

"Where are you now?" Betta asked.

"At the stairs. I hear something upstairs."

The tension in the room was so intense the black cat, who'd been sitting perfectly still, was perched on the edge of the sofa, gaze fixed intently on Duke.

Liza closed her eyes, praying that the whole thing would soon be over. It was unbearable, revisiting the scene of a grisly murder with the man she loved—the man everyone else suspected was the murderer.

Betta's voice was strong yet tender. "Liza, you asked to know this. Do you want to continue?"

She couldn't speak, but she nodded yes.

"Where are you, Duke?"

"I'm at the bedroom door. Something isn't right. The lights are out here. It's getting dark, and Marcelle had purchased a Tiffany lamp for the upstairs hallway. She said she hated a dark hall and that the light would always be on."

Duke knew too many details of Marcelle's taste, her whims and fears. Liza felt as if her heart were being torn as she learned about the small quirks that made up the personality of a woman who was vivacious and exciting, a woman Duke had known far too well.

"Go into the bedroom," Betta directed.

"The door's open. Marcelle is—No!" The last word was a shout. In his chair in Betta's living room, Duke flinched, almost falling over. His hands went up to protect his head. "No! No!" he yelled.

Suddenly, he went limp.

Liza was on her feet, her arms around Duke to hold him as steady as she could. Betta, too, rose from her chair, but she merely gazed at both of them.

"What's wrong with him?" Liza demanded.

Betta put a reassuring hand on Liza's back. "He's fine. He's lost the thread of the past. Now he's merely resting. He's going to be okay in a few minutes." She went to a small cabinet and pulled out a cigarette. "Do you mind if I smoke? I don't often indulge, except in very intense moments. This is one."

"Is he really okay?" Liza knew she sounded like a worried mother. Duke was slumped over, but his breathing was regular. Whatever had confronted him from the past, it was no longer pursuing him.

"Don't be disappointed if he doesn't remember this," Betta warned her. "Using your necklace, I was able to tap into the subconscious, but it doesn't mean he'll consciously remember anything he said."

"But it's there?"

"Yes, it's there." Betta turned away from her. "We should have another session soon. Liza, now don't get upset, but it wouldn't be a bad idea to have some plan should this go the wrong way. It might also be best to keep him in the dark about what you learned tonight."

"Because he knew Marcelle?"

"It troubles me," Betta said. "For you. I can feel your love for him. And his for you. There's no doubt about that. But love isn't a cure for anything. Just remember that.''

"Can you wake him?" Liza asked.

"Yes, I just have to snap my fingers."

When she proceeded to do so, Duke sat up straight and looked around. "I told you it probably wouldn't work. But thanks for trying."

"We had some success, Duke," Betta said, putting a hand on his shoulder. "I'd like to try again. Tomorrow."

Duke looked at Liza. "What do you think?"

"Yes," she said, her heart breaking even more as she realized that this was the first time she'd ever held anything back from the man she loved. She had no choice, though, if she ever wanted to find the truth.

MIKE STOOD IN FRONT OF one of the pen-and-ink drawings and stared at it. The portrait was so intensely personal he felt as if he were privy to Liza's emotions. "I don't know what to say." He looked around the room at all the other drawings. Liza had been very reluctant to show him what was behind the door, but Familiar had kept pawing at it.

As soon as Liza opened the door, the cat had disappeared again, and Mike was left with dozens of drawings of himself.

He studied a dark portrait, his face half in shadow in a darkened alley. It was a picture about hidden sides and secrets. Liza hadn't known about his amnesia or suspected involvement in a murder, but the portrait captured all of that, and more.

"There's really nothing you can say," Liza said, still not moving into the room.

Mike watched her out of the corner of his eye. Liza

had, if truth be told, been upset since they'd left Betta's. She'd told him that he'd spoken of parts of his childhood and had, in fact, referred to the pendant he was holding in his hand when he awakened. The thought of his grandmother was sweet and intense, but it offered no insight into what had happened to him in 1995. The only thing he'd really gained from the hypnosis was hope. Hope that the past would emerge from his subconscious. It was progress that no other professional had been able to offer him.

He looked at the drawings that gave back his own image. It was incredible that Liza had spent so many hours drawing him. The work spoke of many things— her loneliness and love. And the pain he'd caused her.

"Pascal thought I was obsessed," Liza said. She still stood in the doorway.

"I can see why," Mike admitted with a wry grin. "I'm sorry, Liza."

"For what?"

He turned to look at her because she was trying so hard to interject a light note in her voice. She was also failing miserably.

"Whatever happened to me, no matter what it turns out to be, I'm sorry that you suffered."

She shrugged one shoulder. "I'll pour us a glass of port. Do you still like it?"

"I'm sure I do," Mike said, following her into her kitchen. "Since Betta regressed me back to my childhood, why didn't she take it further? We don't have a lot of time to waste. Eventually, the police are bound to decide that I'm a high priority."

The small crystal glass Liza held in one hand slipped from her fingers and crashed to the floor. Glass splinters flew over the room.

"Let me clean it up," Mike said, going straight to the broom and dustpan in the pantry. He looked at them, and smiled wryly. "My subconscious, at least, is working." He swept up the debris, then turned to Liza. "You seem a little edgy. Are you okay?"

"Overly tired." Liza got another glass and poured the port.

"You were about to tell me why Betta didn't push harder," Mike said as he dumped the glass shards into the garbage.

"She did."

Mike finished cleaning up and looked at Liza. "What happened?"

"You were in Marcelle's house, going into her bedroom, and you began to yell, 'No!' Then you slumped over."

He could see that she was reluctant to tell him any more and once again he was reminded of her bravery.

"So I was in Marcelle Ricco's house." That fact made him feel defeated.

"Based on what you said, and it was pretty detailed, you were quite familiar with the layout of the house. You knew about the plans for her party."

He heard the raw pain in Liza's voice. More than anything, he wanted to pull her into his arms and try to convince her that whatever had happened in the past, it had nothing to do with his feelings for her.

But that would be a lie. The past had everything to do with Liza and their love. If it turned out that he'd betrayed her, or cheated on her, she wasn't the kind of woman who could forgive such a thing. Whatever he'd been in the past, he wasn't the kind of man to accept such actions now.

"While I was there, was Marcelle alive?" It was one of the hardest questions he'd ever had to ask.

"I don't know." Liza handed him the glass of port. "It wasn't clear. It's an assumption on my part and one I want to believe. But it sounded to me like you were attacked as you tried to enter Marcelle's...bedroom."

"Will Betta put me back under?" She had to! It wasn't fair that they'd stopped. He could have continued. They'd been on the brink of discovery and it was vital that he learn what happened.

"Tomorrow evening. She said it works better in increments."

"Good." Mike felt like a calf tangled in barbed wire. No matter which way he tried to turn, something held him back. He couldn't remember the events that might redeem him. And if he didn't remember soon, he was afraid it was going to cost him the one thing that he couldn't afford to lose—Liza.

*THE HYPNOSIS WASN'T a ripping success, but progress was made. Listening to the sequence of events through the highly trained ears of a P.I., I'd say that Duke Masonne was set up by a professional. First he's called to the scene and KO'd, then taken to the train depot and dumped in a boxcar!*

*I'm sure the intention was that he die in the boxcar, but he didn't. We need a freight schedule from 1995. Bother, this is going to be a tough one. And to tell the truth, I want some food. Something grilled and delicate with lots of butter. These two are so tense, if they had springs, they'd both pop. So I'll rely on the old phone book and make them take me to dinner. It has to be somewhere secluded yet swank. Mike/Duke can't afford to be seen, and a lot of fancy places don't allow cats. A stupid policy, but I can't change it.*

*Let's see. The River Queen. Live zydeco band, fresh oysters, seafood grilled, fried, sautéed and raw. Sounds perfect. And it's over in the section of town called The Black Pearl. Mike/Duke will be safe, and dinner will provide a diversion that's much needed by these two.*

*There has to be a way that I can make Liza hold on to her faith for just a little longer. The fact that Duke was in Marcelle's house and headed for her bedroom was a severe blow to her trust factor. A good sign is that she decided to listen to her heart and trust him with all the details of the session. Still, she's afraid. Not hard to understand why, but she has to hang in there.*

*I look at her and I see the toll the past five years have exacted. While Duke has been riding the range as Mike, oblivious to what he's missing, Liza has been pining away, hoping for a miracle. The miracle walks in the door and what she gets for all of her waiting is the image of him walking into another woman's bedroom. Eeeyow! Not exactly what I'd call just compensation.*

*So, I've got their attention, and Liza is looking at the yellow pages where I've made my selection. The relief on her face is almost palpable as she suggests going out for dinner.*

*Ol' Mike/Duke is relieved, too. He knows he's messed up, but what can he do? It's a sticky wicket, as a British kitty might say.*

*Some food, some wine and a bit of lively music ought to help. If that doesn't do the trick, I'll have to think of something else. One thing I promise. Mike/Duke* won't leave here tonight. He'll stay if I have to stage a brain seizure. I'm afraid if Liza lets him go, she might not have the courage to hang on any longer. Once they're fed, relaxed and in the sack together, I'll feel reasonably certain they can work out their differences. There's too much love and too much passion between them to just let things slip away.

Off to dine! For an amnesiac cowboy and an artist may work from sun to sun, but Familiar's work is never done.

## Chapter Twelve

Liza woke up with a start, her heart pounding. In the dream, she'd been running down a cobbled street, the bricks wet from a recent rain and slick-looking beneath the streetlamps. Behind her, a dark shadow had followed, a man whose face was hidden by the brim of a hat. No matter how hard she ran through the foggy night, he was always the same distance behind her.

Her neck was tight and sore. She'd fallen asleep sitting in a chair, unable to relax after Duke brought her home from the restaurant and quickly left. He'd been in such a hurry to get away that Liza was left with a feeling of abandonment. And confusion.

Of all the times she'd needed him to take her in his arms and reassure her, last night had been at the top of the list. But he hadn't. And Liza knew it was because he was as troubled as she was.

There was also the fact that Liza's home might still be under surveillance. They hadn't detected anyone following them to Betta's, or back, but that didn't mean Trent Maxwell had given up on capturing Duke. Far from it, if Liza knew him at all. It was rather amazing that she hadn't heard from him. Her thoughts had been so wrapped up in Duke that there had been no room for anything else. Based on recent events, that wasn't about to change.

The session with Betta and the things that had been revealed tormented her. In the weeks and months and years she'd known Duke—had loved Duke—he'd never mentioned Marcelle Ricco. He often talked about his buyers, but her name had never passed his lips.

That was something Liza couldn't overlook no matter how hard she tried—and she had tried. All through dinner, with Familiar to entertain them, she'd held her doubts at bay. Alone, though, she was confronted with too many possibilities. If he hadn't outright lied to her, he'd still deceived her by omission.

"Meow." Familiar nuzzled against her leg and she picked him up and held him. The regular rhythm of his purr was comforting and she buried her face in his sleek black fur.

"I owe Eleanor for leaving you. I think I'm going to have to figure out a way to keep you here with me for the rest of our lives," she said. "So tell me, what should I do now? I just don't know. I can't believe Duke did anything so terrible, but it seems that each passing day shows me something I didn't know about him."

"Me-ow," Familiar said, eyes wide and curious. He put his head on her chest, exactly where her heart was. Very gently, he butted her.

"Trust my heart." Even as she said it, she couldn't help but smile. If the cat wasn't giving her sound advice, he was certainly making her think of it herself.

Trust her heart. That's really all she had to go on anyway.

She thought about the dream, the man following

her. It couldn't have been Duke because the man in the dream had been so sinister. He didn't walk or run; he floated behind her, always able to stay twenty yards away.

She got out of the chair and stretched, walking to the bedroom window that opened onto the balcony. The sweet smell of a blooming mimosa tree drifted up to her through the open window and she stepped through it onto the balcony.

The city unfolded beneath her. In the distance, she heard the jazzy sound of a trumpet playing in a club. Laughter floated on the breeze, the sound of fun. It was all so distant and removed from what Liza was experiencing.

She was about to turn to go back inside when she noticed the slight shift of movement in the alley across from her building. It was the same alley where Familiar had led her to speak with Duke.

Her skin prickled and the hair on the back of her neck seemed to rise a little in anticipation of trouble. Someone was in the alley. Watching her.

To avoid letting on that she knew she was being watched, she forced herself to sit down in one of the wrought-iron chairs that were traditional in New Orleans, especially for balconies. She had enough plants to give her cover.

The idea that someone was spying on her made her furious. She had half a mind to go down there and confront whoever it was. While it would be gratifying, it would also be very foolish. A wiser woman would wait to see what happened. For once, Liza decided she'd be wise.

She sat very still and watched the alley. The shadow was restless. It wouldn't be that long until dawn and

Liza determined to stick it out. She wouldn't be able to sleep anyway. After slipping back inside, she found her sketchbook and began to work. The bright patches of reflected light on the cobbled street reminded her of her dream. As she worked on drawing the dark alley, a creepy sensation sent goose bumps dancing across her skin.

When she looked up, the shadow in the alley had emerged. Trent Maxwell stood on the sidewalk. One hand rested on the gun she knew to be in his pocket, and he rubbed his jaw with the other.

Liza stopped drawing and froze. Trent was the man from her dream. Sure, he said he cared for her, but wasn't standing in an alley and watching her essentially the same as stalking?

There was the whole issue of Duke. Trent suspected him of murder. But had a warrant actually been issued? Or was Trent acting as a vigilante? Because…he loved her? He wanted to protect her?

Slowly, she lowered the pad to the floor. Once again, her impulse was to confront him, but common sense prevailed. She backed into her apartment and away from the windows. It would be far better if he never knew she'd seen him.

Whatever he was up to, instead of making her feel safer, she felt more threatened. And before the morning was over, she intended to have some answers, and Pascal Krantz was just the man to help her get them.

LIZA WAITED UNTIL NINE before calling Pascal, though it almost killed her to delay. At best, Pascal was not an early riser. When he was awakened, he was even more difficult than normal. One thing Liza knew she needed was his cooperation. She'd just gotten him on the phone when she heard the downstairs buzzer.

Portable against her ear, she went down to the ground floor. Duke was easy to identify as he stood outside the glass door, staring in at her.

Her brain might tell her to use caution, to protect herself, but her heart sent another message altogether. The sight of him made her pulse race. How many times had she dreamed of this moment?

Opening the door for him, she motioned him to silence as she relocked it and heard the gruff voice of a sleepy Pascal.

"Your profile was supposed to run this morning. I've got the paper and I need a cup of coffee," Pascal said.

"Sorry to wake you," she said into the phone, her gaze on Duke. He was watching her with curiosity. "I want you to tell me the truth, Pascal. Why is Trent Maxwell watching my home?"

"You woke me up to ask such an obvious question? To protect you. What's this all about?"

Some of the sleepiness had left Pascal's voice, but an undertone of annoyance had crept in. There was the sound of newspaper pages rustling.

"I want it stopped," Liza demanded.

"Then call him up and tell him so. Your finger isn't broken, is it?"

"He won't pay any attention to me. I want you to call him, Pascal."

"Since you've awakened me and since you've taken it upon yourself to decide what I should and shouldn't do, I'm going to give it back to you in spades. Duke Masonne is a suspect in a murder case. If you were behaving like a grown-up, Trent wouldn't have to be watching you. It's because you're acting like a juvenile with a rush of hormones that he feels it necessary to keep you under surveillance.''

"I've taken care of myself for most of my life,'' Liza countered hotly. "When did I suddenly become the source of all this care and worry?''

Pascal had grown impatient. "When you started seeing Duke behind every bush in town. It was bad enough when we thought you were losing your mind. Now, since it turned out you were right, it's worse. Leave him alone, Liza. This isn't going to end well.''

"What do you mean?'' Liza flashed a look at Duke that made him tense. His brow furrowed as his gaze searched her expression.

"The police are about to launch a manhunt. The investigation into the murder of Marcelle Ricco has been reactivated. Trent's been named the head of the search team, and he intends to turn this city upside down until Duke Masonne is in custody. So stay out of it, Liza. You've done yourself enough damage.''

She was astounded although she knew she had no reason to be. Pascal had never cared for Duke, which hadn't kept him from using Duke's high profile and list of wealthy clients to push her career forward. Now, though, it seemed Pascal wanted to see Duke tried, convicted and hanged. "What have I done to damage myself?''

"Have you forgotten your little interview with Anita Blevins?'' He didn't give her a chance to answer. "I haven't. And you won't once you see today's paper. The headline pretty much sums up the story— Prominent Businessman Wanted in Murder Investigation—Local Artist Protects Lover. There's an old photo of you sitting in La Madeleine with Duke.''

"You don't even sound surprised." Liza was shocked, and she held up a hand as Duke came toward her. The concern on his face had deepened, and Liza felt a rush of anxiety at the angry intent that accompanied it. Duke had always been a man with a temper, but he'd always kept a firm hold on it. Or so she'd believed in the past.

"I'm not surprised," Pascal said, his anger making his words rush out. "I didn't expect anything else from *you,* but I was hoping Duke would have enough sense not to embroil you in what can only be a real mess. If he cared anything for you, he'd leave you alone."

"He didn't—"

"Public restaurants, public places. First he stalks you and now he drags your reputation through the mud. Liza, I can't manage you if you're determined to thwart me at every turn. This is damaging. Right now, your audience base is New Orleans and this area. Anita Blevins, for whatever reason, has done a hatchet job on your career."

Liza felt the bottom drop out of her stomach. With everything else going wrong, she didn't need to worry about her career or Pascal jumping ship.

"I can't help what she wrote," she pointed out. "From the moment we sat down to talk, she was on me about Duke. I didn't tell her anything." She knew she sounded defensive, and when she looked into Duke's eyes, she saw that he fully understood what was happening even though he could only hear her end of the conversation.

"I'll do what I can. Maybe we can spin this to show your compassion for an old friend."

Liza was familiar with the calculated tone in Pascal's voice. As much as she hated the idea of "spinning" an act or situation, it was the way the game was played. "Do what you can."

"Promise me that you'll stay out of the limelight. Don't go anywhere in public with that man. Stay away from him, Liza. If you're on the scene when he's arrested, there won't be anything I can do to help you."

"I always thought notoriety worked in an artist's favor." She was trying to lighten the mood.

"It can. If you're a man and if you're willing to take it to the extreme. Neither of those things applies to you. Stay away from Duke and remain in your gallery. It might be nice if you made yourself available should some customers drop by. Even though this newspaper article is awful, it might draw one or two curiosity seekers. I'll be by this afternoon after I've had a chance to talk with the Sunday editor. We happen to be close friends and maybe he can help plug some of the holes Anita blew in our ship."

"Thanks." She put the phone down and stared into Duke's brown eyes. "I'm afraid it's bad news," she said.

"Your career is being ruined because of me?"

She shook her head. She had no intention of discussing that with Duke. None. Pascal's concerns were legitimate, but if success meant abandoning Duke, she would remain obscure. "Trent Maxwell is about to issue a warrant for your arrest. They're reopening the murder case and you're the number-one suspect. They're going to organize a city-wide search."

Duke slowly rubbed his chin, a gesture Liza remembered well. He only did it when he was thoroughly frustrated.

"This isn't fair to you," he said. "I have to leave."

She crossed in front of him and made sure the door was securely locked. "Not this time, Duke. I couldn't bear it if another five years passed before I saw you again." Despite her doubts and fears, she found that she was smiling up at him. A tentative smile at best, it was true. Above and beyond the trauma of what was happening, just looking at Duke made her feel a surge of happiness. "You're not going anywhere without me," she vowed.

"Liza, you should protect yourself. What if—"

She shook her head. "I know you were in Marcelle's home, headed into her bedroom. I know that. I've spent most of the night thinking about it. And Familiar told me something important."

"The cat?"

"He's the culprit." Her smile was growing. The cat had been right on the money. "He put his paw on my heart and told me to trust it," Liza said. She lifted Duke's hand and placed it on her heart. "Feel that."

He nodded.

"That's a true heart, Duke. In my heart, I know you could never kill someone. Not Marcelle, not anyone. Not unless you were gravely threatened. The evidence may point to you, but I won't believe it. I trust my heart." She moved her hand to his face, slowly feeling the slight stubble of his beard. "And I trust your heart, too."

"Me-ow!" Familiar said, rubbing against both their legs before he went to the counter and batted the car keys onto the floor.

"He's saying this is a lovely little tender moment, but there's no time. We have to get on the move. If a manhunt is under way, we have to do some investigating before it's too late."

Liza was reaching down for the car keys when Duke's hand caught hers. Turning her so that she was close against him, he brushed a curl from her eyes. "I couldn't do this without you. The truth is, if it weren't for you, I'd be tempted to head back to North Dakota."

"You could never do that, Duke. I know you. You may think you could walk away from this, but you can't. Now that you've started, you'll have to see it through to the end. And I'll be right at your side. Whoever did these terrible things deserves to pay."

"I love you, Liza. In another life, Duke may have loved you, but I love you now. For exactly who you are, not what you used to be."

"I've always loved you, Duke. Some things never change." She stood on tiptoe and kissed him gently on the lips. "Let's get busy. Once this is behind us, you owe me five years' worth of kisses."

JOE PEEBLES SHOWED LIZA to a seat and he made no effort to hide his curiosity at her unexpected visit. "Ms. Hawkins," he said, "what can I do for you today?"

Duke had coached her and she was ready. "I'd like to see all the paperwork on Mr. Masonne's estate."

The flicker of concern was quickly hidden, but it had been there. "I'm afraid that's impossible. You have no legal claim to see any of his personal papers. I remember the case well. There was no will, noth—"

"That's because Duke isn't dead." Liza extended the handwritten note. "Read it, Mr. Peebles. Duke is very much alive and he's given me authority to see his personal papers. Now."

"This can't be." Even as he was denying it, the

lawyer took the paper she handed him. "He disappeared without a trace. We held his estate for as long as we could. This is a forgery. It has to be."

"No, it isn't." She hadn't expected Joe Peebles to jump up and down with excitement about Duke's return. She also hadn't anticipated the lawyer's near panic. "Funny, but having Duke back alive is making a lot of people uncomfortable. I wonder why."

"I'm not uncomfortable...just shocked." The lawyer pressed the intercom button. "Margaret, would you bring in the files on Duke Masonne, please?"

"Who benefited from Duke's disappearance?" It was a question that had been growing larger and larger in the back of Liza's mind.

"That's hard to say. His business was sold at a loss, so the buyer benefited."

"And the proceeds?" Liza pressed.

"His share is in an account. They're available whenever he wants them. As you well know, he had a partner."

Liza remained silent until the secretary brought in the file and left it. When the door closed firmly behind the woman, Liza picked up the thick stack of folders. "Who would gain the most from Duke's death?"

"Ultimately, you." Peebles's smile was now shark-like. "You're the beneficiary of his huge insurance policy. You stood to get everything." A calculated note had entered his voice. "Another two years, when Duke could have been declared dead, it would have all been yours."

"I never..." Liza reconsidered. She didn't have to defend herself to this man.

"Mr. Masonne had no relatives. You were the sole beneficiary." He reached into his desk drawer and brought out a pair of glasses, slipping them onto his nose. He lifted a file and opened it. "Yes, Ms. Hawkins, in another two years you would have been quite wealthy."

Once again, Liza forced herself to ignore the jab. "Since Mr. Masonne is alive, I'd like you to make his funds available to him."

"I'd be delighted to do so—when he sits across this desk from me. I'm afraid I can't do such a thing through a third party no matter how many notes you bring in. After five years, I want Mr. Masonne's...presence legally verified. I'm sure you can understand that. I wouldn't be a good lawyer unless I took every precaution for the good of my client."

Liza didn't like Joe Peebles, but she couldn't argue with that logic.

"Where are his possessions stored?"

"Perhaps it would be better if I dealt with Mr. Masonne face-to-face."

Liza rose from her seat. "I'm sure that would be more convenient, but Duke has chosen to use me as his emissary."

"I'm not a stupid man, Ms. Hawkins. I hear talk, especially at the courthouse. I've heard rumors that Duke had suddenly reappeared. I've also heard that he's a wanted man. Is that why he doesn't choose to conduct his business personally?"

"I thought you were his attorney. He paid you enough for your loyalty." It was a statement made in anger and one she regretted the instant it was spoken.

"Loyalty can't actually be bought." His smile widened. "Tell Mr. Masonne he'll need to see me himself. I don't think any judge in the country will look on my actions as anything other than wise and sensible. Mr.

Masonne may be innocent of all charges, but I don't want to get caught in the middle of helping a wanted man escape the law.''

Realizing that Joe Peebles was not going to cooperate, Liza nodded. ''When all of this is settled, I'm sure Mr. Masonne will be more than glad to talk to you face-to-face.'' She turned and walked to the door. As she pulled it open, she hesitated. ''Who bought Duke's business?''

''I suppose I can tell you that since it's on the deed of sale. Kyle LaRue bought out Duke's share in the business. Then he sold it for a very tidy profit, I've been told.''

# Chapter Thirteen

Mike sat in the restaurant, the newspaper he'd bought held up to conceal the bottom half of his face, sunglasses obscuring his eyes. He'd read the same article in the newspaper six times and still didn't know what it was about. His entire attention was on the heavy door with the brass plates that marked the entrance to Joe Peebles's office. Any moment now, Liza would come out.

"Me-ow!"

He handed another strip of bacon under the table to the cat. Familiar, so far, had behaved, but now the feline was getting demanding. And anxious. Familiar ignored the bacon and paced back and forth beneath the table.

"Settle down," Mike said, reaching a hand down to scratch the cat's head. "Liza will be here soon."

Instead of soothing the cat, his talk only seemed to agitate him—and also make the waitress cast a look of deep concern his way. Well, he wouldn't be the first customer who sat at a table and talked to himself. New Orleans was a drawing card for people who were "different."

He signaled for his check, realizing that Familiar

was making him as jittery as a bug on hot pavement. But before he could pay, the black cat darted out from under the table and took off through the open door of the café.

"Where in the hell did that cat come from?" The waitress stood with her hands on her hips. "Animals aren't allowed in here, mister. Do you want to get the board of health down on us?"

"Sorry." Mike left a ten-dollar tip and took off in pursuit of the cat. It seemed that whenever Familiar acted strangely, there was good reason.

He'd just made it to the street when he saw the unmarked cars angle onto the sidewalk. He had just enough time to withdraw into the lee of an old brick building before Detective Trent Maxwell and five uniformed officers hopped out of the cars and swarmed into the restaurant he'd just vacated.

He'd escaped in the nick of time. No doubt his waitress was giving them all the details of what he was wearing.

He slipped out of his jacket, hesitating for only a moment. He'd had it for almost five years, a gift from Gabe and Rachel. He dropped it in the alley along with the newspaper and headed down the street in the direction Familiar had taken. He'd find another place to watch for Liza.

A tearoom provided the perfect place to hide. The arched doorway gave Mike a good view of the street yet obscured him from easy view. He'd just settled in when he saw Liza come out of Joe Peebles's office. As soon as she put a foot on the sidewalk, two uniformed officers came out of nowhere. One on either side of her, they started to escort her toward one of the cars.

"Hey, let me go!" Liza tried to shake them off, her gaze shifting toward the restaurant where she was supposed to meet him. To her credit, she instantly changed her focus.

"Detective Maxwell has some questions for you," one of the officers said.

"Detective Maxwell had better have some answers for me," Liza said hotly. "Take your hands off me."

"I'm sorry, ma'am," the officer said.

"Unless you let me go, I'm going to make you very sorry."

The officer tightened his grip. "Don't make us use restraints. You're wanted for questioning in connection with a murder. If you don't cooperate, we can use necessary force."

Mike's fists clenched in helpless anger. There was nothing he could do to help Liza. She was being arrested because of him! And all he could do was watch. He'd never felt so powerless.

"Trent!" Liza spied the detective as he came out of the café empty-handed. "What's this about?"

Trent nodded to the remaining officers. "Keep searching. He's around here somewhere." Then he turned to Liza. "You're coming downtown. I want Duke Masonne, and you're going to tell me where he is."

Once again, Mike had the urge to rush into the fray, but common sense warned him that getting arrested would be the stupidest thing he could possibly do. He pressed deeper into the doorway of the tearoom. Out of the corner of his eye, he saw the uniformed officers headed his way. They were canvassing the neighborhood, looking for him.

"Me-ow!" Familiar was at his feet, black paw striking at the door of the tearoom. "Me-ow!"

Mike had two choices—to make a dash for it down the street and risk a bullet in his back or to head into the tearoom, which might very well be a trap.

"Me-o-o-o-w!" Familiar struck the door with force.

Mike opened it and he and the cat stepped into the semidarkness.

"Your face is all over the news," a familiar voice said.

He turned to find himself confronting Betta.

"There's a back door into the alley." She held out her hand to him.

He took the keys she offered.

"It's the Mustang. Just don't ding it."

"Why are you doing this?" he asked, already moving toward the back door. The police were headed toward the tearoom and Familiar was already waiting for him.

She shook her head. "I always play my hunches."

"Isn't that rather dangerous?"

"So they add car theft to your list of crimes if you don't bring it back. Go! Quickly! I don't mind helping you, but I don't want to go to jail for my troubles."

"Will you get a message to Liza?"

"If I can."

"Tell her—"

"Marcelle Ricco's house," Betta finished.

Mike halted. "That wasn't what I was going to say."

"It's where you should go," she said. "There are questions there that need to be addressed, past secrets that must be faced."

"Maybe you're right." He had to get out of the

tearoom. There was no time to argue. He could see the policemen not ten yards from the door.

He opened the back and stepped into the alley where a black Mustang was parked. Using the key she'd given him, he opened the door. Familiar leaped into the front seat and in a moment they were pulling out of the narrow alley and into the street.

Mike fought down the urge to rush to Liza's aid. The idea that she was being arrested was infuriating, but he had to hang on to the knowledge that Trent Maxwell was emotionally involved with her. The detective might question her, but he wouldn't do anything to harm her.

"I have to focus on finding out what really happened to Marcelle," he said.

"Me-ow!" Familiar gently patted the wheel. When he kept on driving, the cat's claw gently hooked into his hand. "Me-ow!"

"What?"

With more authority, Familiar hooked the wheel to the right.

"You want me to park?"

"Meow!" Familiar blinked and nodded.

Mike pulled the car into an empty spot. "Now what?"

The cat's golden gaze was fixed on an old building. It took Mike only a moment to realize it was the back of Joe Peebles's office.

"So, you think we need to do our own investigation?" he asked.

"Meow." Once again, the cat nodded.

Mike hadn't really had time to think about it, but it was more than coincidence that the cops had come searching for him as soon as Liza made an appearance in Peebles's office. His old lawyer had obviously ratted him out.

"Yes, I see what you mean," he said.

It would be perfect. The police—and Joe Peebles—would never expect him to return to the scene. Yes, it was time for some answers and Joe Peebles was going to give them.

LIZA PACED THE NARROW confines of the room where the police had parked her and left her for the past hour. She knew that leaving her in the seedy room was a tactic—one intended to break her down. Well, they had another think coming. Instead of making her frightened or worried, it was only making her madder by the minute.

When the door finally opened, she rounded on Trent Maxwell. In three steps she was in front of him, and her palm connected solidly with his cheek.

The look of surprise on his face was gratifying. "How dare you?" she sputtered. "Spying on me, following me, and now having me picked up like a criminal." She realized that a great portion of her anger came because she knew Trent. She'd trusted him and had even been allowing herself to grow fond of him—as a friend.

"I dared because I care about you," he said, one hand reaching up to touch the red imprint of her palm on his face. "You have a funny way of saying thank-you."

"Let me out of here."

He shook his head. "Liza, I know you're caught up in this business because of the past. I'm here to tell you that Duke Masonne isn't the man you thought he was."

"I won't listen to this." Liza started toward the door. She didn't believe that Trent would actually charge her with anything. This was all a bluff.

"Open that door and I'll have you put in a holding cell."

Something in his voice warned Liza that he wasn't bluffing. Astounded, she dropped her hand from the knob and turned to face him. "Why are you doing this?"

"Because I care what happens to you."

"Because you think you're a better judge of what I need than I am?" She had to somehow make Trent see that his way of caring went beyond what she could accept.

"In this particular instance, I think the answer to that is yes." He started to approach her but then stopped. "Did you ever stop to ask yourself the question of why I was able to charge Duke Masonne with murder? Remember, five years ago, he wasn't charged."

Liza hadn't given the legal implications a thought, but she found she was listening intently to what Trent had to say. "Go on."

"I wasn't involved in the original case. If you recall, no one was ever charged in Marcelle's murder." He waited for her to nod. "Duke was the prime suspect, but once his car was found in Austin, destroyed, the assumption was that he'd met with foul play."

She nodded again, watching Trent very closely. He seemed intent on telling her the facts, but she had to wonder what his motivation was. Had Duke become a target of a trumped-up murder charge because of her?

"The *assumption*—" he put strong emphasis on the

word "—was that justice had been served. Duke had killed Marcelle and someone killed him."

"Duke didn't kill—"

"Just let me finish. It goes deeper than that, and I want to be honest with you."

For the first time, Liza felt a chill of apprehension at what Trent might tell her. Her stomach tightened and she had the urge to run out of the room before she could hear more. The expression on his face—half remorse and half victory—frightened her. "Finish, then. Just don't drag it out," she said, not knowing how much longer she could force herself to listen.

"It turns out that my predecessor on the case was obligated to several local politicians."

"What does that have to do with Duke?"

He stepped closer to her, one hand going out as if he meant to touch her, but he didn't. "Those politicians were involved with Marcelle."

"Involved…" She frowned. She suddenly understood his meaning. "She provided girls for them."

"Yes. And their friends."

"How cozy." She couldn't help the bitterness.

"Cozy and more than a little hot. It seems that Marcelle was a woman with a fondness for photos and money."

"She had pictures?"

"And she wanted money not to show them around town."

Liza felt the knot in her stomach getting tighter. "I still don't see what this has to do with Duke."

"When Marcelle was killed, a lot of people were very happy. Not the least were the politicians who stood a chance of being exposed if an investigation into her murder was launched."

Liza put a hand behind her and found the door so that she could use it as a support. She felt as if her knees were turning into jelly.

"My predecessor decided the most politically expedient route was to drop the entire case. As I said, the assumption was that Duke killed her and then someone killed him. A full-scale investigation would have damaged his friends." Trent adjusted his jacket. "When I asked to take over the case, I made a few enemies."

"Trent, I understand what you said, but I still don't see what that has to do with Duke. There's no more evidence than there was five years ago."

He finally touched her, both hands on her shoulders as if he meant to support her. "But there is. Liza, I don't take any pleasure in telling you this. You were always straight with me about your feelings for Duke. There was blood in his car. Samples were taken but never tested. It wasn't his blood. It was Marcelle's."

Liza was glad of his hands. She felt her legs trembling and couldn't stop the sensation that her entire body was turning into something less than bone and muscle.

"No," she managed. "That can't be true."

"It is true. Her blood was on the back seat of his car."

A storm of conflicting emotions seemed to rage in her head, but she forced herself to think. Something wasn't right with the scenario that Trent was painting.

"I don't believe this. If Duke could remember, he'd be able to explain."

"Don't you think his loss of memory is just a little too convenient? I mean, he found you. He remembers loving you, but he doesn't remember anything else? That's a little hard for me to swallow.''

''Stop it!'' Liza wanted to put her hands over her ears and block out everything Trent was saying.

''I won't stop it, Liza. You're aligning yourself with a murderer. You don't even know who he is—you didn't know five years ago. Face it, you've been in love with an illusion.''

''Stop. Don't say anything else.'' Liza twisted free of his grip. The one thing Trent had accomplished was to make her angry enough that she was no longer weak and trembling. On the contrary, her mind was in high gear. ''How did you find us at Joe Peebles's office?'' She saw instantly that he didn't want to answer that question. ''Did he call or were you following me again? I saw you in the alley. The way you're watching me makes me feel...violated.'' She saw that her words wounded him, but she didn't care.

''I have been following you. And I'll continue to do so if I believe you'll lead us to capture Masonne. I won't apologize for doing my job.''

''I believe you want Duke to be guilty whether he is or not.''

''That isn't true. If I didn't believe he was guilty, I wouldn't be so motivated to bring him to justice. And if I wasn't worried about you, I certainly wouldn't be staking out your gallery on my off time.''

Instead of gratitude, Liza was only more determined to prove to Trent that he was wrong. ''I thought Marcelle's body was found in her home. It doesn't make sense that blood would be in anyone's vehicle. Even if Duke were the murderer, he'd hardly be so careless as to get her blood in his car. Was the body moved?''

Trent's mouth hardened into a straight line. ''There

are facts about the murder that were never released. I can't talk about them. We'll use them when we prosecute Duke.''

''You tell me horrible things about the man I love and you mix it all with lies. Then you want me to believe you. It doesn't work that way, Trent.'' She walked to the scarred and battered table that was the only furniture in the room and sat down on the edge of it.

Trent followed her and his voice was low and urgent. ''You believe everything Duke Masonne tells you. He conveniently disappears from your life for five years. When he returns, using an improbable case of amnesia as an alibi, you don't even question it. I'm a police officer and you doubt everything that comes out of my mouth.'' He shook his head. ''It hurts, Liza.''

His last words took all the wind out of her sails. Even her anger deserted her, leaving her feeling empty and more alone than ever. ''Please, would you take me home?''

''Tell me where Duke is.''

She could tell by the hardness of his voice that no matter what his personal feelings were, he would do his duty. Or what he perceived as his duty. ''I don't know.'' That was the honest truth.

''That answer won't get you out of here. We can hold you for twenty-four hours for questioning.''

Liza shrugged. ''So hold me. I don't know where he is. He was supposed to be waiting for me in the café across the street. I'm sure he saw you arrest me and he left.''

''Where is he staying?''

''I don't know that, either.'' If he had good sense,

he would be finding a new place to stay. Somewhere safe.''

''Why did he come back to New Orleans?''

''You won't believe me, so why should I waste my breath and your time?''

''Try me.''

''He had my business card. He wanted to find out about his past so he could move forward into his future. It bothered him that he couldn't remember. So he came to find me, hoping that I would be able to tell him who he'd once been.''

''How very romantic. He suddenly looks you up after five years.''

''He finally realized he had to resolve his past to really get on with the future. That isn't so hard to understand.''

Trent went to the door and opened it. ''Go home, Liza, and stay there. If you see Masonne, I advise you to call me. He's a dangerous man. If he doesn't injure you physically, an affiliation with him will certainly damage you professionally.''

''You sound like Pascal,'' Liza said as she walked by him into the dingy green hallway.

''We both care what happens to you,'' Trent said just as she was passing him.

She turned to look into his eyes. ''I'm sorry for all of this. I do care for you. I…'' She hesitated because it seemed no words were adequate. ''I never misled you about my feelings where Duke was concerned. I only wish you weren't involved in this case. Duke didn't kill her, Trent. He didn't. If you're so all-fired determined to find someone guilty of her murder, why don't you check into Kyle LaRue? He's the one who benefited financially from Duke's sudden departure.

Have you ever considered that maybe someone set Duke up?''

Trent's sigh was deep. ''I would give everything I have if you felt strongly enough to defend me against all evidence. It makes me sick to realize how much you're going to be hurt when this all comes crashing down.''

# Chapter Fourteen

Thankful for the dark-tinted windows, Mike eased the black Mustang into the small parking lot. Familiar, front paws on the dash, watched intently, letting out a small meow as the tall man in the suit came out of the rear exit of the building, got into a Lexus and drove away.

"That has to be Joe Peebles," Mike said.

"Meow." Familiar looked at him.

"Okay." He lightly pressed the gas, allowing a car or two to get between him and the Lexus.

When Liza had left the lawyer's building, she'd come out empty-handed. It had been a long shot to send her in to get information, but Mike had been shocked when the police suddenly swarmed the area. It wasn't tough to figure out that Joe Peebles had somehow notified the cops that Liza was there. Taking that train of thought one step further, Mike figured it stood to reason that Joe had something to hide.

As he followed the Lexus through the heavy French Quarter traffic, Mike chafed at the fact that he couldn't remember a thing about the lawyer. Had he and Joe Peebles had a cordial relationship or one fraught with deals and counterdeals?

Probing into his past business dealings was risky. He might learn more than he wanted to know about his ethics and the people he'd willingly done business with.

The truth was, Mike was sick of the specter of the past looming over him. Whatever he'd done, he was ready to confront it. The past five years on the cattle ranch he'd had few opportunities to manipulate high-rolling business deals. There'd also been long nights of poker with the stakes getting pretty high for ranch-hand wages. To his credit, Mike had had no compulsion to cheat his fellow workers.

He couldn't help but feel that a man's essential nature was inherent. Either he was honest or he wasn't; he was a liar or he wasn't. Amnesia wouldn't "cure" a man of dishonest impulses. Hands tightening on the wheel more from his thoughts than the frenetic traffic, Mike held on to the belief that even though he couldn't remember the past, he was still the man he'd always been.

And he wasn't a murderer.

He felt the cat's head bumping his elbow and he released his grip on the steering wheel. Only then was he aware of how tightly he'd been grasping it. With his free hand, he scratched Familiar's chin. The black cat flopped onto his back for additional pets.

"You're a real sucker for a few good scratches," he said. He'd never have thought it possible, but the cat made him feel better.

While he'd been in North Dakota, he hadn't had a pet. The dogs on the ranch were working animals, as were the horses. And the bunkhouse was barren of all pets since the ranch hands were out so often rounding up cattle, helping with the birthing of the calves and tending to other ranch chores.

"When all of this is settled, I'm getting a cat," he said, his hand moving over Familiar's sleek coat. "I'd like to keep you, but Liza said you already have a good home."

Familiar caught his hand with both front paws, then gently bit his fingers.

"Better pay attention. We're headed out of town."

The Lexus was several cars ahead, going under the elevated interstate and headed toward I-10 East. Mike pressed firmly on the gas and the Mustang responded with a burst of speed. In a matter of seconds, he was climbing the concrete ramp behind the lawyer, headed out of New Orleans.

The vista of the traffic and the city sprawling beneath the highway gave Mike a moment of concern. In North Dakota, the vast open landscape had seemed so comforting. Here, he felt as if every inch of space was crawling with life. It was almost as if there wasn't enough oxygen for everyone. Had he worked in New Orleans because it was the only place he knew?

He'd never considered himself a philosophical person, but Mike suddenly realized that his years in North Dakota had given him a chance to experience a completely different life. When all of this was over and his name was cleared, he could stay in New Orleans and pick up the threads of his life as Duke Masonne, or he could go back to Gabe and Rachel and the ranch. He had options that few men were ever given.

The only requirement was that wherever he went, Liza Hawkins would be at his side. If her art, which was so inspired by New Orleans, required her to remain in the French Quarter, then he would stay with her. If not—the wide-open spaces of the north country could become his permanent home.

That thought made him slightly more optimistic as the little black car sped over the lengthy span of the Lake Pontchartrain bridge. Out on the water, sailboats of all shapes and sizes cut through the whitecaps. The wind was up and the lake, though shallow, was vast.

"Shallow," he said aloud. Where had he learned that fact? And it was strange, but he had the sense that he'd sailed before. There was almost the impression of the rope in his hand. He'd taken to using a lariat with great skill—Gabe had even commented on the fact that his hands had worked with a rope before. Had he been a sailor?

Following Joe Peebles, Mike tried to open his mind to the scenery that flashed by the car window. When Peebles took the exit for a town called Slidell, Mike followed.

There was nothing extraordinary about the town. A four-lane highway—jammed with traffic—seemed to be the main artery of the city and the lawyer's destination. It wasn't until Mike saw the beautiful art deco building that he began to suspect exactly where he was going.

The Lexus pulled into the parking lot behind the building. Mike slowed the Mustang at the sign—Kyle LaRue, Exotic and Elegant Imports.

There were small differences, but the design of Kyle's building was more than a mere imitation of the offices Mike had created. They were a direct rip-off. As he closely examined the structure, Mike's feeling of betrayal was visceral. He forced himself to calm down. He wanted to walk in the building and begin throwing punches until someone gave him some answers. Maybe Kyle had a reason for what he'd done, but Mike couldn't think of a legitimate one.

The thing that held Mike back was the sure knowledge that it would take only one phone tip to the police and he would be behind bars. It wasn't worth getting caught to risk the satisfaction of a confrontation.

No, it would be better for him to pull into the grove of willows on the west side of the building and watch. He noticed that, other than the Lexus, the parking lot of the building was empty except for an SUV that more than likely belonged to Kyle.

Mike had the distinct impression that his old buddy and his lawyer had somehow managed to benefit from his "death." He didn't hold it against them that they'd made money—as long as they hadn't done it at his expense.

He was prepared for a longer wait, but Joe Peebles came hurrying out of the building after he'd been there only a few minutes.

The lawyer got in his car and tore out of the parking lot as if the hounds of hell were on his heels. Instead of following the lawyer, Mike decided to take a chance that Kyle would be alone in the building. If he caught his old partner by surprise, he might be able to pry more information out of him.

Leaving Betta's car in the grove of willows, he quickly made his way across the parking lot and slipped to the back. To his relief, the door to the warehouse was unlocked. He entered the dimly lit area and was greeted by the smell of waxed wood. Moving carefully down the aisles, he found the door to the main building. Once again, he opened it without a problem.

The interior office space was plushly decorated, a

gradation of grays and blacks that reminded Mike of photographs he'd seen in magazines.

He moved down the hall toward what he thought would be the private offices. He paused at a closed door, opening it gingerly only to find an empty office. Moving down the hall, he saw a brass plate with Kyle's name on it. The door was slightly ajar.

It opened with the gentlest shove. For a split second Mike thought he had lost his mind. There was no other way to account for the horrible scene in front of him.

Kyle LaRue was sprawled across his desk. The knife that protruded from his neck was ornately carved, the handle a work of art.

LIZA KNEW THE UNDERCOVER officers were hot on her trail, but she forced herself to walk slowly past the café where Duke had been waiting for her. Though she hadn't expected to find any trace of him, she was still disappointed—and anxious.

She had two choices. To go home and wait for him to contact her, which could prove really dangerous for him since she was being so closely watched. Or she could go and talk to Kyle LaRue herself. Kyle's name was the only bit of information she'd obtained from Joe Peebles.

She was about to hail a taxi when a woman stepped out into the street.

"Liza!"

She recognized Betta instantly and hurried through the traffic to join her on the sidewalk. It took only a few seconds for Betta to tell Liza what had happened in the tearoom.

"I lent him my car," she concluded, "but I don't

know where he went. Later, he'll be at Marcelle Ricco's house.''

"Thanks." Liza gave the psychic a hug. "I don't know why you were willing to risk lending your car to Duke, but I thank you."

"He may not remember his past, but he hasn't changed. You have to believe that. I spent a lot of time thinking about what was revealed in the hypnosis session. People don't change. Or maybe I should say seldom change even when they really want to." Betta's smile was wry. "Even after five years, your love for him has remained constant."

"I know," Liza admitted. "Most people would say that I'm a fool."

"Most people never risk truly loving another person." Betta nodded toward two men who'd stopped on the corner and were consulting a map. "You have a tail."

"I know." Liza avoided looking at the two men. She didn't want them to realize she'd spotted them.

"I don't have another car, but I do have a back exit and that will give you a bit of time to hail a cab."

Liza grasped Betta's hand and gave it a gentle squeeze. "I don't know why—"

"I don't, either. I just believe in you and your fella. I'll do what I can to detain the posse."

"Don't get in trouble." Liza was worried that she'd pull an innocent person into the nightmare she found herself in.

"I can manage. Now come on inside and I'll show you the back way."

As Liza and Betta moved toward the tearoom, the two policemen began to follow. Liza knew if she wanted to make her escape, she'd have to act fast.

Once they were inside the shop, Betta showed her the rear exit and she took off down the alley at a trot. If she used a few of the shortcuts she'd learned and stayed off the main streets, she should be at Canal in a matter of minutes. There were plenty of cabs there. Joe Peebles had said Kyle's business was in Slidell. She didn't have the name, but it couldn't be that hard to find an import business in a small town. Even if it was hard, she had to do it. Kyle LaRue owed her and Duke some answers.

She hailed a cab in record time, but the driver was reluctant to take her over the lake. Holding two fifty-dollar bills, she caught his eye in the rearview mirror. "How's this for a tip?" she asked.

"Okay, lady," he agreed, blending smoothly with the traffic that was headed for the interstate.

Once on the highway, Liza could do nothing except watch the miles roll by. On the lake she saw the sailboats and wondered what had happened to Duke's twenty-footer, the *Bonnie Ann*. He'd enjoyed sailing and had been good at it. Funny, but she hadn't even thought of the boat in years.

As soon as they got over the bridge, she directed the driver to pull into a small café. The place was filled, and Liza hoped that it would be like most busy eating places in small towns—the center of all gossip. Her hunch proved correct, and after a two-minute conversation with the woman behind the register, Liza knew exactly where to find Kyle LaRue.

The cabdriver was anxious to return to New Orleans, so Liza got out in front of the building. She simply stared at the structure, which was an exact duplicate of Duke's office near the docks.

She'd never involved herself in Duke's business,

just as he'd never meddled in her art. They'd done the necessary social events—for each other. On one or two occasions, she'd met Kyle LaRue and at no time had she ever believed he was mentally unbalanced. But the building before her told her otherwise.

He'd re-created Duke's dream office—and claimed it for his own. It was surely a form of madness. Had Kyle taken it far enough to murder someone and then frame Duke?

Suddenly, Liza realized that she was in a very vulnerable position. The parking lot around the building was empty except for a solitary vehicle. That in itself was strange. LaRue's place should have been open for business.

Goose bumps skidded across Liza's upper arms, and her fingers went to find the pendant she wore beneath her apple-green silk shirt. She'd intended to confront Kyle, but now that didn't seem like such a smart plan.

In the near distance she heard the wail of a siren and was reminded that she'd barely escaped the two New Orleans cops that Trent had sent to follow her. Either she was going to go in the building or not. She had to make a decision and get off the street.

Before she could decide, a streak of black shot from the side of the building and headed straight toward her. "Familiar?" It didn't seem possible, but she recognized the black cat.

"Liza!" She looked up to see Duke waving to her from the shrubs beside the building. "Come on!" He didn't wait but started across the parking lot. Galvanized by sudden fear, Liza ran toward him.

"The car's in those trees," he said, pointing to the willows where the black Mustang was almost invisible.

"We need to talk to Kyle." Liza reached out to grasp Duke's sleeve and stop him.

"It's too late for that. Kyle's dead."

"What?" Liza wanted to stop, but Duke grabbed her hand and pulled her after him.

"He's dead. Someone stabbed him."

Liza balked, but Duke was stronger and managed to keep her jogging.

"I followed Joe Peebles over here. He came running out of the building, and when I went in, I found Kyle LaRue dead."

They'd reached the car and Duke hurried her into the passenger seat. Familiar hopped into her lap as Duke ran around and got in on the driver's side. The sound of the sirens grew steadily louder.

"We have to get out of here," he said. "The cops are on the way."

"What happened to Kyle? Who stabbed him?"

Duke already had the car in motion, but he applied the brakes and turned to look at her. "I didn't kill him. Is that what you're asking?"

"No." But Liza realized her answer wasn't exactly accurate. "Maybe. I don't know." She felt the tears well in her eyes. "How is it possible that he's dead?"

"I don't know." Duke stepped on the gas and headed west, away from the oncoming sirens. "I walked in and he was lying across his desk. He'd been stabbed in the back."

"What are we going to do?" Liza looked out the rear window of the car in time to see three Slidell police units roar up to the building. "They know what's happened. Look at them. Someone called them."

"It could have been Peebles. He went inside and rushed out as if he was being chased by demons."

"Do you think he killed him?"

"I don't know," Duke answered. "What I do know is that once again I find myself at the scene of a murder. Only this time I know I didn't do anything wrong."

"We can't afford to be seen anywhere near here." Liza's impulse was to put as many miles between her and the scene of Kyle LaRue's murder as possible. "Kyle bought out your business and then sold it for a big profit. That's the one thing I learned from Joe Peebles." She didn't have to add that it would also be considered a strong motive for Duke to kill Kyle.

"It's obvious to me that my lawyer and my friend were working together."

She heard the disappointment in his voice, and it reminded her that Duke Masonne had never been a man who would trade friendship for profit.

"Duke, maybe we should go to the police."

"Me-ow!" Familiar's cry was strident.

"Familiar and I both disagree with that," he said. "Someone set me up for Marcelle Ricco's murder. That someone is still on the loose. If I did something wrong, I don't mind paying the price for my actions. But I don't want to go to jail for something I didn't do." He paused. "Did you get anything else from Peebles?"

"Nothing useful." Liza remembered something she'd learned. "Marcelle was an art collector. You said her friend mentioned that she was somehow involved in underhanded art deals."

"That's right."

"Would you mind if I looked in her house? There may be something there."

Duke pressed harder on the gas and the little sports car responded with a surge. "That's a brilliant idea, Liza. Whatever I once knew about art, I can't remember. There may be something in her house that you'll recognize. I believe Lisbeth will let us look."

Liza closed her eyes for a moment and tried to regain her composure. It seemed everything she held dear was unraveling around her. Her hand slipped across the console and lightly touched Duke's thigh. Whatever obstacles she had to surmount, she would do it. With Duke beside her, she could do anything.

"Meow." Familiar nuzzled under her chin.

"And you, too," she said softly to the cat. "We're going to figure this out," she said with conviction. "We're going to find out who killed Marcelle, clear your name, and then we're going to have a life together."

Duke's answer was to lift her hand to his lips and softly kiss it.

# Chapter Fifteen

As he pulled the Mustang into the driveway of Marcelle's Garden District house Mike felt as if his skin had been peeled back revealing raw nerves. He was keenly aware of Liza's every motion. He saw the rapid intake of her breath as she steeled herself for the confrontation with the past—and with her own fears.

She believed in him; he didn't doubt that for an instant. But he also knew that her belief was based on the trust she felt for a man who was gone—a man he didn't remember. Worse than that, he couldn't even offer her the comfort of wholehearted denials. He didn't *believe* he'd killed Marcelle Ricco. But, dammit, he couldn't even remember that!

Frustration gnawed at his gut, and he got out of the car with a swiftness that implied a plan of action. It only hurt him more to see that Liza eagerly followed his lead. It was a case of the blind leading the blind.

Only the black cat, who hopped out of the car and made his way up the gracious front steps, seemed to have any real idea of what to do or how to go about doing it.

He knocked sharply on the door and was relieved to hear the sound of someone moving within the house. There was a crash, the sound of glass breaking, and his hopes faltered. Lisbeth Dendrich was a hard-drinking woman. How reliable was anything she had to say going to be?

Liza had the same concerns. He could see them on her face. Just as the front door swung open, he saw her shoulders square and he felt an intense pride. She was one helluva woman. Western women prided themselves on strength of character and the bold determination to persevere against all odds. They fought weather, hardship, isolation, and a life where disaster or death lurked in drought, flood, famine and snow. Yet Liza Hawkins was their equal in every way. She had heart, spirit, intelligence and talent.

His attention was diverted from Liza to the woman who opened the door. Lisbeth Dendrich was standing, but barely, as she swung the door wide. Her gaze focused on him and her smile was welcoming. Then she saw Liza, and her expression shifted to one of examination.

"So you're the woman who tied Duke's heart in a knot." She caught hold of the door for balance. "Come on in before the cops see you standing out here and arrest all of us."

Her words caused Mike to glance toward the street. There was no sign of the police, but that didn't mean they weren't around.

"Have the cops already been here?" Liza asked.

"Yes, and they refused the drink I offered." Her eyebrows arched. "That was a mistake. I hate to drink alone." She waved them inside and closed the door solidly behind them. "Welcome to Casa Ricco."

She said the name with a hint of malice that Mike didn't miss.

"I would think by now you'd view this as your home, not Marcelle's," he said carefully.

"It's hard to lay claim to a place that's haunted by the former occupant." Lisbeth's laugh was harsh. "I have the perfect reason to drink—I'm haunted!"

Mike exchanged a look with Liza, telling her with his eyes just to wait and listen. She was strung tight, and he tried to reassure her with his expression.

"If my balance were better, I'd serve drinks, but since I'm doing pretty good just to remain standing, why don't you follow me to the kitchen so I can make us something?"

"Ms. Dendrich, Lisbeth, I'm in a lot of trouble. I—"

"Don't I know it. The cops threatened to take me to jail for obstructing justice. I told them to get the paddy wagon but be sure to lay in a good stock of Asti. I can drink anywhere, and at least in jail I'd have someone to drink with."

Her words were flip, but Mike heard the pain beneath them and he knew that Liza heard it, too. Still, he was surprised when Liza stepped forward and touched Lisbeth's arm.

"If we can find out what really happened to Ms. Ricco, maybe we can find some peace for all of us. For Duke, for me, and for you."

The gentle kindness seemed to take Lisbeth aback. Her gaze lingered on Liza and then shifted to Mike. "I see now why you don't want to risk losing her."

Without another word, she pushed through a big oak door and led them to the kitchen where she pulled a fresh bottle of sparkling wine from the refrigerator.

"Do the honors, please." She held it out to Mike.

He took it, popped the cork and filled the three glasses she'd put on the table.

He knew Liza didn't want to drink—neither of them could afford the luxury of befuddled mental capacities. They both knew how to hold and sip a drink, though, and Mike felt a burst of renewed hope that he remembered even that small detail. It was something from his past life, a tiny something to be sure, but a chink in the wall of amnesia that held him prisoner.

"What are you looking for?" Lisbeth asked.

Liza spoke up first. "Marcelle's body was found…" She faltered, looking from one to the other. "There's no easy way to say this. You found your friend here, in her home. Is that correct? I mean, she was killed here, right?"

"In her bedroom." Lisbeth waved vaguely toward the upstairs. "I'm not likely to forget that scene. Blood everywhere."

Mike spoke to Liza. "What's this about? There was never any question about where the body was found."

"When I was being detained, Trent told me that Marcelle's blood was found in your Land Rover."

"What?" Mike and Lisbeth spoke in unison.

"That's what he said. They did the tests, and blood smears in the back seat of your vehicle matched Marcelle's."

"I read every article about Marcelle Ricco's death. There was no mention of blood smears or samples or tests." Mike found that he wanted to pace, but he forced himself to stand at ease, the champagne flute in one hand as he allowed himself a puzzled expression. "If I had killed her, would I be stupid enough to leave her blood in my car?"

"That was exactly what I pointed out to Trent,"

Liza said. She turned back to Lisbeth. "Was there a chance the body had been put in her bedroom?"

Lisbeth's face reflected her horror at the memory. Mike knew then that she was indeed haunted—by what she'd witnessed or was somehow a party to. For the first time he noticed that Familiar had slipped into the house with them. The cat was sitting quietly under the kitchen table as if he were drinking in every word Lisbeth Dendrich spoke.

"The place was drenched in blood. The police told me at the time that she'd died in that bedroom." Her voice lowered to just above a whisper. "That's why she's still here, still lurking around. She wants her justice, and she thinks I've let her down because I haven't found out who killed her." She stopped talking and looked at Mike. "Unless, of course, it was you and you're here to finish what you started."

The words were so matter-of-fact that Mike found it hard to trust his ears. "You don't seem afraid of me. Of us," he pointed out.

"At this point, death would almost be a relief." Lisbeth drained her glass and refilled it. "You're thinking—is it guilt that's turned this woman into an alcoholic? The answer is yes. Guilt and a vivid imagination. How many times a night can you witness a murder scene in your dreams before you get up and reach for the only thing that seems to dull the images?"

"We aren't here to judge you," Liza said quietly, once again making Mike realize how much he admired her quiet courage and generous compassion. "We're here asking for your help."

"Ask away." Lisbeth topped off her glass.

"We want to look at some of Marcelle's art collection, what there is left here, and we need you to recall any pieces that might have been removed.''

"I didn't have the judgment Marcelle had. She could walk into any gallery and head immediately to the most valuable work of art. She had a real eye. That's why she trusted you, Duke. She said you never inflated the value of a piece and that you took only an honest commission for finding it.''

"Nice to hear,'' Mike said. "Will you walk through the house with us?''

"It would be helpful if I knew what, in particular, you were looking for,'' she said.

"There was a watercolor, a young girl on a porch. She's looking around a column.''

"Yes.'' Lisbeth nodded even as she began to walk. "Right this way.''

They found the painting in the front drawing room, and Liza stood before it for a long moment. Mike didn't recognize the painting, but he easily identified the style as Liza's own unique talent.

"It's one of yours, isn't it?'' Lisbeth asked, moving closer to examine the signature.

"Yes.''

Mike watched Liza, sensing that something was wrong. "What is it?'' he asked.

"Pascal told me that Marcelle bought this painting. She helped Pascal sell several of my early works, according to him. It's just odd, the way all these different things come together in this house.'' She shivered slightly and stepped away, moving on to a Picasso that hung on another wall. "She kept me in good company,'' she said, then gasped.

"What?'' Mike was instantly at her side.

"This Picasso. I think it's a forgery.''

"How can you tell?" Lisbeth asked, suddenly more alert than she'd seemed before.

"If I'm not badly mistaken, the original work is in a private collection in Germany. It just happens that I read an extensive article about how the painting was recovered from a discarded bundle of canvases in the back of an old building. When it became apparent that it was a masterpiece, it sold for close to a million. The buyer made a big deal out of how it would be his and only his. It sparked a debate in the art world about private versus public collections."

"Are you sure?" Mike asked. He wasn't certain what this meant. He only knew that he was a little closer to figuring out the mystery of Marcelle Ricco's death.

"Yes," Liza said firmly. "This picture is a fake. And from what we've learned about Marcelle Ricco, she must have known it was fake."

Mike nodded, then turned back to Lisbeth. "I need to ask you some questions about Marcelle's body."

Lisbeth blanched, but she waved her champagne flute with nonchalance. "So ask."

"Would you mind showing us exactly how you found her?"

"I mind a helluva lot, but somehow I don't think that really matters to you."

Mike touched her arm. "It matters. If I could make all of this go away—for both of us—I would."

"Yeah, okay," Lisbeth said grudgingly before she turned to lead the way up the stairs. "It was in the bedroom, like I showed you before." She hesitated at the threshold, collected herself and walked into the room. "She was there, in the bed. She was dressed up for some occasion. She looked beautiful—except there was blood all over her dress. It had soaked into the floor.'' Her voice quivered, but she continued, ''The knife was still sticking in her throat.''

''Throat?'' Mike said the word in disbelief. The grisly scene of Kyle LaRue's murder was still vivid in his memory.

''She'd been stabbed in the chest and in the throat. The knife was left in the last wound. It was a knife she'd ordered from India. Very elaborately carved.''

''Exactly like LaRue,'' Mike said. ''But wait a minute. Marcelle Ricco was stabbed in the heart. That's what the newspaper accounts said.''

The look Lisbeth gave him was one of speculation. ''Is that amnesia talking or innocence?''

''What do you mean?''

''Well, the account of her murder was deliberately distorted—the type of wounds were kept secret. It was part of the police ploy to help weed out the crazies who called in and confessed to the murder.''

''What?'' Mike shook his head in astonishment. ''The police deliberately lied about the murder scene?''

''You got it,'' Lisbeth said, her nervous gaze moving to the now immaculate bed again and again. ''They said Marcelle was beautiful, glamorous, a celebrity. Her murder would draw a lot of wanna-be killers. They used the press to mislead the public so that when these wackos called in, they would give the details of the murder they'd read in the newspaper.''

''Clever, but they could have simply withheld the details,'' Mike said. ''I'm beginning to have grave concerns about local law-enforcement policies.''

''You and me both,'' Lisbeth agreed. ''But you say that you know only what you read in the papers. The

problem is that it might be because you're innocent—
or that you simply don't remember.''

"Back to square one," Mike grumbled with more
than a hint of frustration in his voice. "Did you
know?" He turned to Liza and realized that she was
as pale as a ghost. Her hands were trembling so that
she had to put down her glass of wine. "Liza?"

"I'm fine. We should go," she said, her voice
shaky. "Thank you, Lisbeth. We certainly appreciate
everything you've told us."

"Thank you," Mike added, taking Liza's arm. He
didn't understand what had shaken her so badly. She'd
read the account of the murder in the newspaper. The
image of the knife in the throat was gruesome, but any
murder was a nasty business.

"Let's go downstairs," Lisbeth concurred, obviously eager to leave the bedroom where her friend and
benefactress had died.

"You've helped more than you know," Mike said,
almost supporting Liza out of the bedroom and down
the stairs. "Thank you."

"If you need anything else, just call."

"You wouldn't happen to remember some details
about the knife, would you?" Mike had questions
about Kyle LaRue's murder. He, too, had been
stabbed. And the knife had been ornate, a ceremonial
knife rather than the standard murder weapon.

"Better than that, I have a photograph. Marcelle had
everything in her house insured. It was one of the
things I did for her—made sure a professional photographer came by to document her art pieces. No doc-
umentation, no insurance payoff if it's stolen."

As she talked, she went to a cupboard in the drawing room. Pushing it aside, she lifted an antique rug

and revealed a floor safe. "Duke, if I thought you were a murderer or a thief, I'd be more cautious." She worked the combination and in a moment drew out a thick sheaf of pictures. "Here." She handed an eight-by-ten glossy over to him.

Mike inhaled sharply. "Are you certain this is the knife?"

"Positive. I'll never forget a detail of that scene."

He felt Liza move closer to him to examine the photograph. She hadn't seen Kyle LaRue's body. She wouldn't recognize that a duplicate of the knife—or possibly the same one—had been used in the murder of the importer.

"I'm assuming the police took the knife for evidence?"

"As far as I know, they still have it." Lisbeth's eyebrows drew together in a frown of concentration. "What's going on here? What's the significance of the knife?"

"Do you know if she bought it from me?"

"That would be my assumption. As far as I know, she used you exclusively for that type of piece."

"Again, thank you." Mike knew now where he needed to go and what he needed to do. He'd been neatly framed for a murder five years in the past and he'd stumbled into another frame in Slidell. But the real criminals had made a serious mistake. If the murder weapon found on the bodies of Marcelle Ricco and Kyle LaRue was indeed the same one, then somebody in the New Orleans Police Department had to be directly implicated.

"Liza, are you ready?" he asked.

"Yes."

He gave her a sharp glance. She was too pale and

too quiet. "Lisbeth, do you mind if I keep this picture?"

"Help yourself. The negatives are in a vault in the bank. I doubt I'll ever recover the knife anyway. Evidence in old cases has a way of disappearing. Or so I've been told."

"Yes," Mike said, guiding Liza out the door. "So I'm beginning to discover.

He looked around for the cat. Familiar had completely disappeared. Maybe he was outside waiting.

He escorted Liza into the car, ready to burst with the pieces of the puzzle he'd put together. The biggest problem was that the man most likely to be the culprit in his scenario was none other than Trent Maxwell. The man was Liza's friend. Possibly a very false friend, but it was going to hurt her nonetheless.

As soon as he was behind the wheel, he turned to her. "Are you okay?"

"Marcelle was stabbed in the throat."

The statement was made in a monotone that instantly made Mike turn his full attention to Liza.

"Yes. That was a startling bit of information."

"When my apartment was broken into, there was something I didn't mention."

Mike shifted so he could put both hands on Liza. He felt the need to comfort her, to somehow share physically with her his newfound confidence that the case would be solved. "What didn't you tell me?" he asked gently.

"I told you that someone had stabbed the antique pen into your portrait. I didn't mention that it was in the throat."

Mike had never before felt dread creep into his bones. Liza's words, though, had the effect of chilling him through and through. "My God, Liza, the killer was in your apartment."

"Do you think the same person killed Kyle LaRue?"

"I haven't figured all of it out, but we're getting closer." He stroked her sunstruck hair, wanting to pull her into his arms but restricted by the car's console. "We'll find the truth," he said. "I swear it, Liza. I know I'm innocent. I can see a pattern of entrapment at work here. Five years ago, I was set up to walk into Marcelle's house and have a murder pinned on me. Those same people are free and they're getting more and more desperate."

"The killer was in my home." Liza's tone was flat.

"You can't stay there any longer. We'll put you in a hotel, someplace safe."

"What are you going to do?" Flatness was replaced by anxiety.

"Instead of the mouse, I'm going to be the cat." He grinned at her. "I've been led around by the nose ever since I got back in town. Well, enough is enough. We're going to be the one setting the traps from now on."

"Meow!" The black cat leaped through the open window and landed on Liza's lap. He looked at Mike and blinked twice.

"Familiar agrees," Mike said.

"You have a plan?" A hint of excitement edged Liza's voice. He could see that her spirit was reviving. She'd had a bad scare and a lot of ugly realities brought home. But she was a woman of tremendous strength and now she was once again showing her mettle.

"First on the list of prey is Joe Peebles. And I need your help to lure him into the trap."

"Squeak, squeak," Liza said. "Just call me bait."

# Chapter Sixteen

*Because so much of this case depends on the trust that Miss Renoir and Mr. Unforgettable develop between themselves, I've done my best to take a back seat, intervening only to steer them in the right direction. But they are only humanoids. It's time for the master chef to stir the pot.*

*The question that intrigues me most is why a woman of Marcelle Ricco's exquisite taste would have a fake Picasso hanging in her house. She had plenty of money to buy the real thing, and if not a Picasso, she had an eye for new talent. Her money would have been far better spent on an unknown artist with a shot at a future career. That was the game she played in other instances—buying and then reselling new artists once their reputations were established. So why the Picasso—a picture that's fairly easily identifiable as a fake? She knew better.*

*The symbolism of being stabbed in the throat is also something my humanoid friends haven't considered. Liza is an artist, and I think I can communicate this concept to her if I discover evidence that shows I'm on the right track.*

*What is in the throat? The larynx, of course. The*

*voice box and vocal cords. It isn't normally the target of choice for a murderer. The heart, the lungs, the carotid artery in the neck, but that's generally a slashing cut, not a stab wound. No, someone was leaving a very clear message. Shut up! That's exactly what it means.*

*And the picture of Duke, also stabbed in the throat. A copycat act? Possibly. A coincidence? Not on your life.*

*There were no fingerprints in the apartment. This alone isn't a valuable clue. Plenty of burglars are smart enough to wear gloves. But this wasn't a burglary. This was an act of intimidation, a warning, perhaps even a clever trap.*

*The lock on Liza's apartment window was broken, yes, but there wasn't a sound. I was there. Now I've been known to exude a few kitty snores, but never while I'm on the job. I sleep like I walk—lightly. I'm willing to stake my P.I. career on the fact that Liza's apartment wasn't actually broken into. I believe the damage to the window was done while Liza and I were gone. Then someone slipped in, savagely stabbed the drawing as an act of intimidation and left the pen in an attempt to tie it into the past.*

*I've given it considerable thought, and what woke me up was the sound of the paper ripping when the pen was stabbed through it. Not a loud sound at all, but enough for a black cat who's always on the alert.*

*As to the mysterious reappearance of the antique pen, that's potentially the best clue of all.*

*If I had to pull out the pieces of this puzzle that related to the antique pen, Marcelle Ricco would be the biggest and best piece. The pen is exactly the type of historic objet d'art that would have made Marcelle salivate. The pen is beautiful, artistic, of historical value—in other words, perfect for her. The only problem is that she's dead. Unless her ghost brought it over to Liza's apartment and left it as a calling card, someone else had to do it. And where did she get it? From Duke?*

*A vital piece of information is where that pen has been for the past five years. I don't buy the theory that it "fell" out of Liza's desk just at the moment the intruder needed a symbolic weapon to destroy the drawing of Duke.*

*So far, too, no one has made anything of the fact that Liza's new style of painting was destroyed. It's almost as if the intruder was sending a message—shut up or maybe shut Mike/Duke up. Couple this with the destruction of Liza's art and I see someone with a strong need to control Liza.*

*I want to pay a call on Betta. She's a woman who would understand symbolism. I'll have to trust that Liza and Mike/Duke can manage by themselves for a few hours. Mike/Duke has a plan and Liza has angst. Well, I can solve this case or baby-sit. Since I've chosen not to have feline offspring of my own, my answer is obvious. Adiós, amigos. The Lone Familiar rides again.*

LIZA PACED the plush carpet of the hotel room Duke had asked her to rent under an assumed name at the historic Monteleone, a place that held many romantic and wonderful memories. It was an elegant suite, and the beauty made her own thoughts that much more difficult to bear.

While Duke had found hope in the details of Marcelle's murder, she had not. The memory of the pen stabbed through her drawing of Duke frightened her now more than it had when she'd discovered it. The malice of that act made her realize that the killer they were trying to bait was a person who delighted in great cruelty. Someone who was mentally unbalanced and capable of anything.

To keep her mind from running in circles, she clicked on the television and found the evening news focusing on the murder of Kyle LaRue in Slidell. The police had worked quickly in connecting LaRue to Duke. When Duke's photograph flashed on the screen, she sat down on the bed, unwilling to trust her legs to support her. All stops had been pulled. Duke was now a prime suspect in two murders.

As head of the investigation, Trent Maxwell was interviewed. Though his demeanor was calm and contained, his words were inflammatory. Duke was portrayed as a dangerous criminal, a man who'd thrown over a privileged past for a life of power and money.

Listening to Trent talk, Liza had the feeling that she'd never really known him at all. He'd always seemed so compassionate, so willing to listen to all sides before he rushed to judgment. In Trent's mind, though, Duke was a dangerous murderer, and he didn't hesitate to paint that picture on the newscast.

Instead of getting better, things were only getting worse.

When the segment on Duke was over, Liza turned down the volume and looked up the number to Betta's tearoom. The psychic answered on the third ring, the first question out of her mouth as soon as she heard Liza's voice concerning their safety.

"We're fine," Liza reassured her. "Duke is still

using your car. He asked me to phone you and let you know it was safe and that he'd make it up to you."

"That's fine," Betta said. "There was a man looking for you. He said he was your manager."

"Pascal?"

"Yes." Betta's voice held a note of caution. "He was with a police officer. Trent Maxwell. Liza, they knew you'd been here. I'm pretty sure they're checking out my car. Duke needs to be careful."

"I know." Liza did know, but there was nothing she could do.

Duke was gone. Convinced that Joe Peebles was working with the police, Duke had gone to use a pay phone to call the lawyer and set up the trap.

"Tell him when he's finished with the car to leave it in the parking garage at the Royal Sonesta. I'll say it was parked there all along. The attendant there owes me a favor or two."

"Thank you." Liza sighed deeply. "It seems for the past two days all I've done is thank strangers for helping me."

"And you, in turn, will help others."

Liza's laugh had a degree of humor in it. "You make everything sound so logical, as if it's just a matter of time before I regain control of my life. I only hope you're right."

"You'll see. Now, this Pascal, he said he was very worried about you?" She ended her sentence as a question rather than a statement. "I couldn't exactly put my finger on what he's worried about."

"Pascal's worried that I'll mess up my career and all his hard work will be for nothing. If I'm labeled some kind of crazy woman, then it may affect my marketability."

"He sounds lovely," Betta said dryly. "I'm glad I denied everything."

"I did make him sound awful," Liza said. "I'm sure Pascal is genuinely worried about me. He's dedicated to my career. He thinks Duke is a mistake. I'm afraid if I tell him anything, he'll go straight to Trent and the police."

"Then it's best to avoid him."

"For the moment, at least. But it isn't right to worry him like this."

"And how is Familiar?"

Liza had been worried about the cat. He'd disappeared at the same time Duke did, but she was growing accustomed to the way he came and went at will. "Working, I think. He left when Duke did."

"I'm not surprised. He's an old soul, Liza. He understands the human heart far better than most people ever do. Take heed of him."

"I will," Liza promised. "I've grown quite fond of him. There's something I want to ask you, though. If we can manage another hypnosis session tonight, do you think you could help us?" Liza hated to put Betta in a position of defying the law. "I wouldn't ask except that I'm certain all the answers are in the past. And we did make headway the last time. I think Duke's on the edge of a breakthrough."

"I think you're right. If he could only regain his memory, he'd know the source of danger—to both of you. Yes, tonight. But not at my house. Can we manage to get into the house where Marcelle Ricco was murdered? That might open the door to the past for Duke."

"We'll manage it. The woman who owns it seems willing to help us." Liza gave Betta the address.

"Good. Then we'll meet at ten o'clock."

"If I can't make it, I'll leave a message for you at home."

"Good enough. Just be careful, Liza. There's something at stake here, something big that none of us fully understands."

THE LAWYER'S DRAWL WAS soft and distinctive of the "uptown" region of New Orleans where the money was old and the names dated back to the Louisiana Purchase. Listening to the polished tones of Joe Peebles, Mike had a moment where he felt he was about to remember something significant. Whatever it was, it slipped away, a shadow in a place of darkness.

"Hello! Hello! Is there someone on the line?" Peebles asked with aggravation clear in his voice.

"I saw you at LaRue Imports. No matter how hard or fast you run, you can't avoid the truth of a photograph." Mike listened to the sound of an indrawn breath and then waited.

"Duke?" Joe Peebles sounded dubious.

So the lawyer recognized his voice. "Surprised to hear from me, Joe?"

"What do you want?"

"The truth would be a good place to start."

"You have no reason to imply that I've ever been anything but honest with you. You disappeared. You left everything in one hell of a mess, and I straightened it out for you. I've taken only my percentage off the top, just like we agreed. I've done everything by the book, but I'm not going to put myself in the middle of anything for you. You're a wanted man—in two murders."

"I know you're trying to keep me talking while

your friends in blue trace this call. It won't work. I'm at a pay phone and by the time they get a patrol car here, I'll be gone.''

"I wouldn't—"

"Save it, Joe. You called the cops when Liza stopped by your office. I don't remember much about you, but I've already learned you're a snitch. Not a good thing for a lawyer.''

"I—"

"Don't try my patience, just listen. I want you to meet me. I want my personal papers showing all the legal transactions that have been conducted since my alleged death. My business was sold, and somehow your little trip to Slidell makes me believe you know something about the details. You and LaRue. And now that LaRue's dead, it seems you're in a pretty tight spot. What happened? Did he try to double-cross you?''

"He was dead when I walked into his office. I swear it. I ran because I was afraid, but I didn't kill him. I didn't—"

"It would be wise of you to be quiet and pay attention. I hear you talking and I hear an echo of myself. I didn't kill Marcelle Ricco. Funny how no one will believe me.

"Should I decide to distribute the photographs I have of you running out of LaRue's building, I don't think anyone will believe you, either. The cops are trying to pin LaRue's murder on me, too. If I give them the photographs, they'll go after you. How would you like to walk a mile in my shoes?'' He let the silence hang for a moment. "Reconsidering your actions, Joe?''

"I am. I never thought…that you might be innocent."

"It never occurred to you that I wasn't capable of killing a woman? Was I such a son of a bitch in business, then?"

"No. Actually, not at all."

"Then why didn't you give me the benefit of the doubt?"

"It was your fiancée's manager, Pascal Krantz. He came by shortly after you disappeared and filled me in on Marcelle Ricco's murder and how you had killed her and fled. I just…it sounded very plausible. Krantz wanted to make sure that Liza's interests were safeguarded and that her name wouldn't come up in any legal proceedings."

"Ah, good old Pascal." Mike was developing an immense dislike for Liza's manager. "A finger in every pie, but mostly a hand clutching his pocket to make sure his money is secure."

"Yes, I suppose you could read his actions that way. This is all his fault. If he hadn't convinced me of your guilt, I would never have considered calling the police."

"Enough. My time is limited and it's clear you're willing to blame anyone except yourself. I'm warning you, Joe, if you double-cross me this time, you'll pay dearly. Have the police been able to trace the call yet?"

"Duke, I don't know. I'm sure the line is tapped."

"They'll have this number any moment. So listen closely. Wait for a call from Liza. She'll tell you exactly what to do." Mike hung up with a feeling of satisfaction. For the first time since coming to New Orleans, Mike felt he was fully in control.

LIZA CHECKED THE TIME. Duke had explained how crucial it was that her call to Joe Peebles followed exactly on the heels of his. She dialed the number and waited anxiously for the secretary to put the lawyer on the line.

"Liza?" Joe said, and she could hear the sweat in his voice. "Duke says he has photographs of me leaving the building. But that won't prove anything. There's no way to prove when I was coming out of the building. His photographs don't prove a thing."

"That's not true, Mr. Peebles. I saw you coming out of the building, too. I was with Duke when he took the pictures. If I were called as a witness, I'd have to tell the truth."

"But I didn't kill Kyle. I didn't. There are some things...Duke deserves to know the full truth. I think if we all sit down together, we can figure this out."

The plan was going exactly as Duke had predicted it would. Confronted with the fact of Duke's innocence—and the feeling of what it was like to be falsely accused, Joe Peebles was coming around.

"Can you pick me up?" She checked her watch again. She'd talk for another four minutes. That would give the police plenty of time to trace the call. The precinct house wasn't far from the Monteleone. They would be after her within the half hour. "We need to talk before the police talk to me. If they ask me, I have to tell the truth."

"The truth is I'm innocent. You have to believe me."

Liza smiled, knowing Duke would be proud of her. She'd been doubtful she could hold up her end of the plan, but everything was proceeding like clockwork. "Duke was very upset with you. He said you'd double-crossed him with Kyle. That isn't true, is it?" Liza flicked her hair over her shoulder.

"Of course not. Kyle bought out the business, and when he had an opportunity to sell it for a big profit, there was nothing I could do to stop him."

"Oh, so he bought Duke out. I'm sure if you explain that Duke made money, too, he wouldn't be so angry."

"Yes, well, the real-estate market was depressed at the time. We had to let the building go at a loss, I'm afraid."

Liza felt her own temper begin to heat. It was pretty easy to keep a dead man from making a profit. "We'll want to look at the documents. All of them. Somewhere there's a clue as to who killed Kyle and Ms. Ricco."

"Liza, I have a house in Mandeville. You and Duke could hide out there for a few days and be perfectly safe."

"How generous of you. Yes, maybe that would be a good idea. You can pick me up. I'll be waiting at the corner of Bourbon and Iberville."

She hung up and walked to the window. Now it had begun. Duke's plan had been set in motion. The only thing she could do now was wait and see if it would play out as he expected.

That and worry that Duke was safe. While she was at risk, he was the one in true danger.

# Chapter Seventeen

As soon as the phone rang, Liza picked it up. "Are you okay?" She thought her heart would pound out of her chest before she heard Duke's affirmative answer.

"And you?" he asked. "How did it go?"

She quickly told him about her conversation with Peebles. "He's going to pick me up at Bourbon and Iberville. He's rethinking your role in all of this."

"Yes, we had an interesting conversation. Joe isn't quite the villain I thought he might be. So now we have to continue. If it isn't Joe, then we have to flush out the real mastermind. So what about the police?"

"I'm sure they're on their way here. They were tracing the call and I stayed on the line plenty long enough for them to get it right."

"Is everything ready?"

"Yes." She hesitated. "Are you sure? Duke, you're already wanted on two counts of murder. I don't think it's a good thing to leave the note."

"I'm positive. Just leave the note and get out of there. Peebles is a lawyer, but he isn't a killer. You'll be safe with him and you'll divert the police from me."

"I made an appointment with Betta." Just to be on the safe side, she couched the directions in ambiguous words. Duke would know exactly what she meant. "The place where it all began. At ten."

"We'll be there together."

Liza gripped the telephone tightly. "Duke, promise me that you won't disappear again."

"Liza, not even hell freezing over will keep me from seeing you tonight. Bank on it."

Liza recognized the term that Duke had frequently used. It was just another little sign that the man she loved was struggling to come out of the darkness of amnesia. Duke was fighting for his life—and his past. All she had to do was believe in him.

"I'll be waiting for you," she said. "I love you, Duke. I always have." The whole plan with the note made her very nervous. If something went wrong, Duke would forever be labeled a kidnapper and a killer.

"There's never been anyone for me but you, Liza. There never will be. Nothing can keep us apart."

"I'll see you tonight." Liza replaced the phone and checked to make sure the note was prominently displayed on the bed.

*I'm a desperate man. Leave me alone or I'll be forced to hurt Liza.*

What Duke had engineered was truly a game of cat and mouse. The police would chase each other—and Joe Peebles—around in circles. The hope was that whoever was guilty would make a misstep that she and Duke could catch. "Apply heat to all sides," Liza said as she rushed down the back stairs of the Monteleone and out onto the street.

She had one personal call to make—one that Duke

had discouraged her from making. But Pascal would be worried sick. He was a bottom-line man, but he was also the only friend she'd had in the past few years.

Pascal's shop was on the way to her rendezvous point with Joe Peebles. She'd just stop in and tell him she was okay.

Liza hadn't gone two feet from the hotel door when she saw the news rack. The photograph of Duke's portrait—the pen-and-ink one with the antique pen stabbed into it—caught her eye. The headline screamed at her—Artist Threatened By Wanted Man. Pascal hadn't been able to keep the police from using her private matters in their war against Duke. It was sickening.

She slowly approached the news rack, remembering Pascal's words. He said he would "put a spin" on recent events in an effort to salvage her career.

"Oh, no," she whispered, noticing that the story carried Anita Blevins's byline. Pascal had sacrificed Duke to try to save her! She didn't bother buying the paper. She started running toward Pascal's, the early-evening humidity making her cheeks flush as she dashed the four blocks to her manager's apartment.

Breathing hard, Liza slowed a block from Pascal's. She was headed toward his front door when it opened. In a golden shaft of light, Anita Blevins stepped into the street.

"Anita darling, the story was brilliant," Pascal said as he hugged the art critic. "Once again, you were a master of understatement and the queen of digging out the ugly truth. Poor Liza. She's fallen completely under the spell of that man. She was obsessed for all these years, and now that he's back she simply can't see him for what he is—a cold-blooded killer.''

Liza didn't wait to hear more. ''That's not true, Pascal,'' she said, walking up to the two of them. She took in Anita's startled look with satisfaction. Pascal, though, was unflappable.

''Liza, you've done everything but take out an ad in the newspaper proclaiming you're unbalanced and desperate for love.''

''Duke isn't a killer.'' Having a discussion with the art critic wasn't part of Duke's plan, but Liza understood the power of the press. She had to stop Anita from writing further erroneous stories.

''Masonne's been charged with the murder of Kyle LaRue. That's the second murder he's wanted for,'' Anita Blevins pointed out with more than a hint of a smirk.

''He's been framed. Again.''

Anita turned to Pascal as if Liza weren't there. ''You're right. She's totally obsessed. It's the artistic temperament. Fabulous for creativity, very impractical when it comes to living in the real world.''

It took everything Liza had not to answer sharply. But Anita wasn't her worry. Pascal was, and she directed her next remark to him.

''As you can see, I'm fine.'' She thought about the fake kidnapping note. But once she made Pascal understand, he'd play along with her. ''I wanted you to know I was okay, but what you've done isn't. It's one thing to try to salvage my career. It's another to do it at the expense of someone else, especially when you know the charges are false. That story will exacerbate an already terrible situation. I hope you're prepared for the consequences of what you've done.'' There was no use arguing with Pascal now. The damage was done. Besides, nothing she said would sway him, and she had more important business to take care of. She started down the street.

"Liza, wait." Pascal caught her arm. "Fire me if you want. I don't care about the job. I care about you. Come inside for a moment."

Liza started to refuse, but Anita Blevins was watching with too much satisfaction. More grist for her newspaper mill. "Duke is innocent," Liza said. "I'm not obsessed or stupid."

Pascal blinked as he stared into her eyes. "I never meant to imply you weren't smart. But you have been under this man's influence even though he's been absent. You have to admit that."

"I don't admit that at all. Duke hasn't influenced me. For the past five years I've worked hard. My career has skyrocketed. Duke had nothing to do with any of it. Now that he's back—and falsely accused—I want to help him prove his innocence. But that has nothing to do with my painting or my career."

"This won't affect your work?" Anita asked pointedly.

"Life affects an artist's work. But hiding out from life isn't the solution. Change isn't always bad, is it? Sometimes it's considered growth."

"Very well put." Anita looked toward Pascal.

"This isn't a topic for discussion on the street like a huddle of gossiping housewives," Pascal said tartly. "Liza, come inside. Anita, I'll set up an appointment with Liza for you, and the two of you can hash this out to your hearts' content."

Liza reluctantly allowed Pascal to lead her into his apartment, a place she hadn't visited in several years.

The first thing she noticed was that he'd completely redecorated. Instead of the Dutch painters that had once adorned his walls, giving his apartment a sense of dark richness, he now exhibited several paintings in the style of the Impressionists. The result was bright with color and light.

"Pascal, I have to go. Duke and I have a plan. In fact, I left a fake note implying that Duke was going to do something desperate to me. You have to play along with it, okay?"

"Certainly. That's an interesting way of proving his innocence. But I have something to show you. Promise me you'll wait here while I get it." Pascal paused in the hallway, waiting for her response.

"I can't wait long."

"I'll just be a moment."

He slipped quickly from the room, making Liza aware once again of his agility when he chose to move fast. To most people he seemed a short, stout little man.

She turned to examine the artwork on his walls. She didn't recognize any of the painters—probably new artists Pascal was representing. The work was excellent, so very different from Liza's own style, but beautiful nonetheless.

She wasn't aware Pascal had returned until he spoke, little more than a whisper, just behind her. "I'm sorry, Liza."

She swung around, her hand at her throat. "You startled me," she said. Before she could react further, he grabbed her arms. He was short, but he was very strong. "What are you doing?" she demanded.

"This is for your own good. Every time you're out of my sight, you end up in more trouble. This way, you'll be safe. Duke is going down for those murders, and I can't let you get tarnished. Your fake abduction will work perfectly."

As he spoke, he was dragging her deeper into the house.

She tried to pull free. "Pascal, let me go." Liza was more astounded than angry. Pascal had always been a man who acted on his whims, but he wasn't the kind to manhandle her.

"I'm doing this for your sake, Liza."

As she saw he was dragging her to a bedroom, she began to truly struggle. "This isn't amusing. Let me go. Now!"

He didn't bother to answer. Using his superior strength, he shoved her into the bedroom and quickly slammed the door. There was the sound of a bolt sliding into place.

Liza grabbed the doorknob and twisted it with all her strength. It was locked.

"Pascal! I have something important to do. Let me out of here now and I'll forget the whole thing."

"You'll be safe here, Liza. You can fire me tomorrow if you wish. But you'll be safe and your art won't become part of a scandal."

"I'll charge you with kidnapping."

Pascal laughed. "I'm afraid Trent will agree with my actions. Kidnapping is rather a strong word to define what I'm doing, which is protecting you. Besides, from what you said, Duke has already taken the blame for kidnapping you."

Panic struck Liza full force. Duke was counting on her. She and Joe Peebles were to lead the cops on a merry chase while Duke gained access to the lawyer's office and files. Duke was certain that he'd find the necessary clues there to figure out what had happened to Marcelle and Kyle.

"Pascal, you can't leave me here."

"You have everything you need, Liza. I'll be back shortly. And by the way, scream if you like. The walls are old brick—three feet thick. No one can hear you."

A chill shot through Liza at those words. He was going to leave her locked in his apartment. No one had a clue where she might be. And if she didn't meet Joe Peebles, Duke's whole scheme would fall apart.

*FATE IS A FICKLE BEASTIE. If I had to guess, I would say that fate is feline in nature. My intention was to scoot over to Betta's. I'd hoped to make a point with her about the symbolism of the stab wounds and what do I find? Anita is visiting Pascal Krantz. Then along comes Liza. Miss Renoir disappears into Pascal's abode and doesn't come out. But Pascal does. Now my choice is to follow him or to discover why Liza remained behind. I suppose since my charge is to protect Miss Renoir, I'd better see what's happening here.*

*These old apartments are always interesting to break into. There's no way to secure every little nook and cranny, and though I've put on a few pounds in the past year or two, I'm still a svelte and slinky puss. There's this lovely little opening just into the laundry room, and voilà! I'm in. And it doesn't take a sleuth to figure out where Liza is—I can hear her screaming.*

*Gads, woman! Save your lungs. Rescue is on the way. I'm going to have to give it all my effort, but finally she hears me. And she's calling my name. Listen to the relief in her voice. She knows I'm here to save her. The only problem is that these old doors work with a very specific key—not the pop-a-lock style of newer, cheaper doors. And it appears that Pascal has removed the key from the lock.*

*Hang on, Liza. Let me look around this place and see if I can find the key. I suppose the logical place would be his desk. What a clutter. This will take forever, and if I don't get busy, Liza's certain to start screeching again.*

*Let's see, there are invoices, shipping labels, bills of sale, newspaper clippings about sales and... Holy moly! I can't believe this! Something is very wrong. Here's an article about Liza's portrait of the little girl on the porch. It says the painting was stolen from one Webster Finch!*

*But that same picture is hanging in Marcelle Ricco's house!*

*Kitty paw on the forehead. How could I have missed this connection? All along, there's been the hint of Marcelle's involvement with stolen goods. But everyone was so busy trying to link it to Mike/Duke that no one thought to look any further—not even me!*

*I have to make Liza understand this. Let me slide the article to her under the doorway. Yes, she has it in her hand and her reaction is a big gasp!*

"My goodness! Familiar, it's my painting and it was stolen. That's odd. Pascal told me that Marcelle bought it, and it's hanging in her home. This means... I've got to make my escape. There's a connection between Pascal and Marcelle."

*Miss Renoir made the correct deductions! Now I have to get her out of here before Pascal returns. Time is of the essence!*

*Uh-oh! The front door is opening! Dang it, he's coming back. And I have to hide. Liza hears him, too.*

*Slide the clipping back out to me quickly. Yes, she understands. I have it now.*

"Don't worry about me, Familiar. Get this information to Trent. You won't be able to find Duke, but take this article to Trent and make him understand, okay?"

MIKE WATCHED FROM BEHIND a Dumpster as Joe Peebles pulled away from his office building. Liza had done her job, luring the lawyer away. Mike knew better than to believe Joe Peebles would help him in any way. But whatever was in his file, he intended to find out.

He slipped up the fire escape and through the office window with ease. Luckily, the heavy oak doors that led to the lawyer's receptionist were closed. Mike tackled the filing cabinets. Figuring out the filing system wasn't difficult and he quickly found the *M*s. Masonne International was a thick file, and he lifted it out. He crossed the room, then made himself comfortable in Peebles's chair as he opened the folder on the desk.

The paper trail wasn't hard to follow. It also yielded no new information except that his business had been sold to Kyle LaRue at a loss. That one fact might imply some kind of illegal conspiracy between LaRue and Peebles; otherwise everything seemed to be in order.

"Damn." Mike shut the folder on another dead end. He'd been certain that his file would contain something that would lead him to the truth.

He heard a car door slam outside the open office window and he went to look out. To his surprise, Joe Peebles had returned. For a moment, he was confused.

Liza knew how important it was to keep the lawyer away from his office. Why would she bring him back? He leaned out on the balcony a little farther.

There was no sign of Liza.

His initial reaction was to slip out the window and make his getaway, but a greater concern for Liza made him remain. Whatever Joe Peebles had done with Liza, Mike intended to find out. After a hasty look around the room, he hid behind the floor-length drapes and waited for the lawyer to return. A few minutes later, the heavy doors opened. Peebles stood there.

"My appointment stood me up," he said to his secretary as he entered.

"Are you okay, Mr. Peebles? You seem upset."

"No interruptions."

Peebles closed the door and went right to his desk. When he saw the Masonne file lying on his desk, he stopped. Then he picked up the phone and punched in a number.

"She didn't show. It was just an excuse so he could search my office." There was a pause. "No, there wasn't anything to find. I told you that. The transactions were all legal and aboveboard." Another pause. "Okay." He put down the phone and turned to look out the window, noticing for the first time that it was open. He walked over to close it.

"Don't bother," Mike said, stepping out from behind the drapes. "I'll be leaving in a little while. Right after you tell me what you did to Liza."

Peebles had started at Mike's sudden appearance, but he quickly regained his composure. "I never saw her." He turned and waved at the file. "Did you find what you wanted?"

"Not exactly. But I'm not interested in anything

except Liza. Where is she?'' Something was very wrong. Mike wasn't certain what, but he knew Liza wouldn't have missed her appointment with Joe Peebles if she could help it.

"I was supposed to meet her and waited for twenty minutes. She didn't show up, so I came back."

"Whom did you just call?"

Peebles shrugged. "Trent Maxwell. I'm working with the police in this matter. In fact, Maxwell is on his way. He'll be delighted to find you here. Save him a lot of legwork. And don't bother with the blackmail attempt. I told Maxwell about going to LaRue's and finding his body. It's all out in the open now, so you don't have anything to hold over my head."

"That almost makes me believe you're innocent, Joe." Mike couldn't help but look at his watch. His whole plan had gone awry. Not only was his file empty of any useful information, but now Liza had disappeared.

"Listen to me, Duke. Turn yourself in. If you truly don't remember what you've done, there's a chance you can get off with a stretch in a mental facility."

"My biggest concern right now is Liza Hawkins. Before I hand myself over to the courts, I think I'd better make sure she's safe." Mike edged toward the window. If Joe wasn't lying and Trent Maxwell was on the way, it was time for him to make an exit.

"As your lawyer, I recommend that you give yourself up," Peebles said. "And give up those photographs. I told the police everything—that I'd been at the scene of Kyle's murder and that you had pictures of me there. The end result is that the photographs will only prove that you were there, too."

"So, you've thought of everything to cover yourself.'' Mike had to give the lawyer credit—he was slick.

"You said something to me earlier, Duke. Something that made me think. You asked me what it felt like to be accused of something I didn't do. Although the evidence is stacked against you, I can see where you may have been framed. If that's the case and if you'll give yourself up, I promise I'll do whatever I can to help you.''

The offer came as a surprise, and Mike didn't bother to hide it. "Why would you do that?''

"You honestly don't remember, do you?''

"Remember what?''

"Six years ago, a client accused me of making advances. Sexual advances. It was all a lie, but the publicity was devastating. Several of my largest clients shafted me even before the case went to court. As a matter of fact, it never went to court because the woman dropped the charges. By then, though, a lot of damage was done. You were one of the people who didn't fire me. You never even mentioned it to me— it was just business as usual.''

"I don't remember." And Mike didn't.

"What you said this morning made *me* remember. It also made me ashamed. I sold your business at a loss. I didn't treat you with the same respect you showed me. But I didn't do anything illegal. What I did was worse. As soon as I spoke with Liza, I called the police. I believed you were guilty without any evidence. Now, the only way I know to help you is to give you the best advice I can. Give yourself up, Duke. Then we can go about fighting this thing legally.''

"Do you believe I'm innocent?''

The lawyer hesitated. "I don't know. But I don't believe you're guilty, if that's a help."

Mike shook his head. "It's not good enough, I'm afraid. I'd love to take your advice, but there's more at risk here than just me."

"Is there something I can do to help?"

Mike hesitated. He didn't know whom to trust anymore. But he did know that Joe Peebles was no longer a suspect in the chain of events that had led to his present circumstances. "I'll give you a call later."

"Be careful," the lawyer said as he watched Mike step through the window.

Mike felt the gun in his rib cage before he'd cleared the sill. He turned to face Trent Maxwell.

"I played a hunch that you might still be hanging around here," Trent said. "Where's Liza?"

"That's what I have to find out," Mike said, wondering if he could ever make the detective believe him.

"This isn't a time for games," Trent said, motioning Mike back inside the lawyer's office. "Two people are dead and you've made a threat against Liza's life. We found your note in the hotel room. It's a clear implication that you've kidnapped her."

Mike felt his hopes sink. The note was designed to lead the cops on a chase. Now that Liza was missing and they had him in custody, it was the most damaging thing that could be found. He'd seriously miscalculated.

# Chapter Eighteen

Liza leaned against the heavy wooden door of her prison and listened to the ringing phone. It sounded as if it were just outside the door—just beyond her ability to get to it. She wanted to pound the door with frustration and yet she knew it was futile. She thumped and kicked the door for half an hour and achieved only sore fists and feet. The door was solid.

During her assault on the door, she'd put together some of the pieces of the puzzle that had become Duke's life—and her own. Pascal was involved in some kind of art theft. That much was clear. He and Marcelle Ricco had been working together to move stolen paintings. Beyond that, she didn't want to go, because if she took this line of thought to its logical conclusion, she knew she would scare herself silly. She was a prisoner in Pascal's home, and no one—except Familiar—knew she was there.

No matter how she tried to keep her thoughts under control, her mind jumped ahead to a frightening realization. It wasn't possible that Pascal was a killer. She'd known him for the past ten years. She'd barely been out of college when she'd met him at a showing of her work. From then on, he'd taken charge of her career, helping her move from being a timid college student to a painter with elegant gallery showings and a presence in the art world.

Yes, he was domineering and a bully, callous and self-centered, but that was what made him such a great agent and manager. Her success meant his success, and he never lost sight of that, pushing for that career dream.

She leaned her ear against the door and forced herself to listen to the telephone conversation.

"Ah, Trent, so good of you to call. No, I haven't seen Liza. She's with that awful man, I suppose. What? You found a note. He's threatening to kill her! That can't be true. Well, if I see her, I'll certainly warn her. Yes, I know you're greatly concerned for her safety. As am I. Thank you for calling."

There was the sound of footsteps coming toward the door. Liza prepared herself to rush out when she heard the lock clicking. When the door swung open, she bolted toward Pascal. "You can't keep me locked in there. I have..." She saw the knife in his hand and knew the metallic taste of fear. "Pascal?"

He shook his head. "Poor Liza, always the innocent. You had a great future, my dear. Such a shame that you won't live to enjoy it. Those who own one of your paintings will see an instant rise in the value of the work. Ironic, isn't it?"

Liza backed away from him into the bedroom. "Pascal, what are you doing?"

"Duke has, once again, made my work easier. How brilliant of him to leave a note threatening your life. I thought I had him in a failproof snare with Marcelle. Circumstantial evidence just isn't enough these days, though. This time, with his leaving the note, there's no doubt he'll go to the electric chair.''

The note was supposed to throw the police off on another wild-goose chase. Now it had backfired.

"You can't mean that you intend to kill me."

"It is a shame, Liza. You haven't really done anything to warrant such a fate except to fall in love with the wrong man. That isn't such a terrible thing. Not like what Marcelle did.''

"What did she do?" Liza had no reason to hope that by delaying Pascal she was doing anything to save herself. No one would think to look for her at Pascal's. Still, she had to try to keep him talking.

"Marcelle got greedy. Greedy and deceitful. That's why she had to die.''

"You killed her?" Liza knew the answer; her mind simply didn't want to accept it. "All these years you've known. And Duke? Did you know where he was?''

"I thought he was dead." Pascal shrugged, the motion bringing the tip of the knife into a shaft of light that made it glitter. "He should have died after that beating. He somehow managed to survive the ride in that boxcar. Who would have thought he'd live all the way to North Dakota?''

"All along it was you. My manager. My friend." Liza whispered the words. She couldn't take her eyes off the knife. It was an elaborately carved dagger exactly like the one that had been used to kill Marcelle Ricco. And Kyle LaRue.

"I made you who you are today. Without me, you would still be a nobody.''

"And you think that makes what you've done okay?''

"Because of me, your paintings become more and more valuable with each passing day. It was a brilliant plan. I would sell them to locals, make sure they were heavily insured, then steal them. Marcelle would then pass them on to some of her European clients at a hefty price tag. She knew how to get them into the hands of private collectors, to minimize the risk that they'd be seen again. It was a very nice plan, until Marcelle became greedy and tried to blackmail me and some of my clients."

"So you stabbed her in the throat." It was as if she'd stepped into a nightmare. A bedside clock ticked softly, a reminder that time was marching forward at a steady pace. Liza felt as though she were stuck in some place where time didn't exist.

"Only after I'd set Duke up to take the fall."

Liza could only stare. "Why, Pascal? Why pick on Duke?"

"He was convenient, and he was also poking into my business. He was beginning to influence you, to encourage you to branch out in your artwork, trust your own judgment."

"And he deserved to be framed for murder for that?"

"You were my creation and he wanted to take you from me."

"And Kyle LaRue?"

"A fool! He was greedy and a coward. Duke's return to New Orleans terrified him. He acted like Duke was a ghost come back to haunt him. After one conversation with him, Kyle was certain Duke knew that he'd cheated him out of his business. He was going to confess his sins and ask for forgiveness."

"He was going to tell the truth, so you killed him, too."

Liza saw the pattern so clearly now. Pascal Krantz simply killed anyone who got in his way or foiled his plans. And the knife he held in his hand indicated that she wouldn't be an exception to the rule.

Liza took a bit of solace from the fact that Trent wasn't somehow embroiled in the web of deceit. It seemed everyone she'd trusted was knotted into Pascal's evil scheme—willingly or otherwise.

"Then it was you who slipped into my apartment and stabbed the drawing of Duke?"

"Of course. Brilliant, wasn't it? And the pen was a stroke of genius. I'd stolen it the day before Marcelle had to be killed. It was exactly the kind of item she would have been able to sell in Europe for me. Once she was gone, I kept it. For sentimental reasons."

"And then it was useful to point the blame at Duke once again. Just like the blood in his car. You put it there, didn't you?"

"Yes. Duke fell in Marcelle's bedroom in some of her blood. When his unconscious body was put in his vehicle, the blood was smeared there, too." Pascal waved the knife. "Come along, Liza. We have to make a short trip."

"I'm not going to make this easy for you."

"You don't understand. What you do or won't do doesn't matter. You can come with me and hope that Duke arrives on his white horse to save you, or you can balk and force me to kill you here. The only inconvenience is hauling away your dead body, but you aren't heavy."

Liza knew by looking into his cold, dead eyes that he wasn't lying. If she balked, he'd kill her where she stood. "Where are we going?" Her only hope was the black cat. Familiar knew where she was and the danger she was in. Once she left Pascal's, no one would know where she'd gone.

"I think we need the perfect scene for the perfect crime. How about Marcelle Ricco's place?" His smile was cool.

"There's someone living there." She hoped to pour cold water on his plan. Anything to delay her fate.

"I wouldn't get my hopes up where Lisbeth Dendrich is concerned. If she's home, she's drunk as a lord. I could host the Riverdance troupe in her living room and she wouldn't hear a thing."

Liza shot a furtive glance at her watch. It was nine-thirty. In another half hour, Duke was set to meet her at Marcelle's. If she could drag out the trip for just a little while, she might have a chance.

"Let's go." Pascal's hand was rough.

"Why did you destroy my painting? You said you liked my new style. You said you thought I was developing a different perspective."

"Indeed. I never lie about art."

"So why did you destroy it?"

"Liza, think about the content. You accidentally witnessed one of my employees making a heist from a very loyal and very wealthy French Quarter client. The possibility that you might actually paint the thief kept waking me up in the middle of the night. You have an uncanny eye for detail, and your drawings of Duke are testimony to the fact that you can sketch a person with the accuracy of a photograph. Yes, you are a talent."

Liza heard Pascal's soft chuckle, and it was one of the most frightening sounds she'd ever heard. The scene came back to her: the man with the canvas, shifting and darting through the crowds. His movements weren't comic as she'd first thought, but furtive. "I can draw him," she said. "But I won't."

"I don't believe you, dearest. I'm not that naive. Once you're out of danger, your conscience will force you to spill everything you know. Through the years I've come to know you well."

"You could have waited for me to finish the painting and then taken it, claiming it was damaged or something." Liza's fear had, for a moment, taken a back seat to her curiosity about Pascal's behavior.

"At first I tried to discourage you, but then when I realized you were working on the painting anyway, I knew I had to destroy it. Duke's return gave me the perfect opportunity to kill two birds with one stone— to incriminate him and to destroy the work."

For a split second, Pascal looked away. Liza knew it might be her only chance. Rushing forward, she pushed him as hard as she could. When he stumbled backward, she fled past him and through the door. She crashed into the hallway wall and then ricocheted out into the foyer. Behind her, she could hear him. As she'd noted earlier, he was fast and agile for such a short, heavy man.

She reached the front door and twisted the knob. The door failed to budge. She jerked it hard with both hands, using one foot to brace against the jamb.

"It's locked," Pascal said from just behind her.

Liza tugged at the door again, this time screaming. "Help me! Please, help me!" Her thoughts raced. She had to leave some kind of clue where Pascal was taking her. If Familiar came back with help, the cat might be smart enough to figure out her destination.

She felt the blow on the side of her skull, and the last thing she remembered was clinging to the doorknob as her body slid to the floor.

*THERE'S NO TIME to track down Mike/Duke. But I do know the fastest way to get some help for Liza. I seldom find a need for any of the limited antics humanoids have learned, but at this moment, speech would be nice. Humanoid speech. Mankind just isn't capable of learning the more complex language of felines, yet the ability to telephone the police would be very useful.*

*Dang these tourists! Not only are they poor drivers, but they can't even walk sensibly. They're clotting the streets and the sidewalks, gawking and snapping photos. I'm swift and nimble, but it's hard to dodge a stumbling herd of cows.*

*At last, the tearoom. And there's Betta, reading cards for a customer. I only hope she's as perceptive as I thought because she's going to have to be very good to understand what I'm trying to tell her. Lucky for me I took the newspaper clipping of the art theft and one of Pascal's business cards, which also includes his home address.*

*God bless her, she's giving her client's money back and sending her on her way so she can give me her full attention. And those blue eyes are focused right on all the stuff I brought her. Now I can paw the art-theft headline and Pascal's name. Yes, she gets it! Now how to tell her about Liza? I know, the phone book. I can point out Liza's name in the phone book and...the tarot cards! There's the death card!*

*She understands that Liza is in danger. Now, one*

*more step. Back to Pascal's business card where I point out his home address.*

*I could sandpaper-tongue this woman's face for a week! She is brilliant. And she's smart enough to call the police. She's even asking for Trent Maxwell. And she isn't taking no for an answer. Trent is busy! Well, he'd better get unbusy. They're patching her through on the radio. She's telling Trent that Liza is in danger at Pascal's home and she isn't answering any questions about how she knows this—a good thing, too, since cops aren't inclined to believe psychics or cats!*

*Liza, help is on the way! It'll be faster for Betta and me to run back over there than try to find a cab in the milling throngs of tourists. Come on, Betta, let's make tracks!*

"You HAVE TO TAKE ME," Mike said softly but with determination. They were still in Joe Peebles's office, and time was slipping away from them. "It's Liza and she's in danger. I know it." He looked at the lawyer. "She would have met you if she'd been able. One thing I know about Liza is that she doesn't leave a job half-finished."

"You know this or you remember it?" Trent Maxwell asked.

"Now isn't the time to split hairs. I told you my story—it's the truth. Whether you believe me or not, we have to help Liza. We've already wasted too much time." Mike knew that his future depended on his ability to maintain calm. Though his heart was racing and his body urged him to choke the facts out of the police detective, if he showed one sign of being unstable or overwrought, Trent would simply call a black and white to detain him. And in that time, Liza could be hurt. Or worse.

"I'm not certain I want you anywhere around," Trent said.

"Liza's in danger. Whatever you have to do, just do it." He held out his hands. "Cuff me to the furniture or send me to jail. I don't care what happens to me. Just make sure Liza isn't hurt." It was a gamble, but he could see that it was paying off. The detective's hard gaze softened.

"Let's go," Trent said.

In moments they were in the unmarked car. Mike gripped the armrest. Trent had the lights flashing and the siren wailing, and if fools didn't get out of the way, Trent showed a remarkable reluctance to slow down. He sent several pedestrians diving off the street and onto the sidewalk. Mike only wanted him to go faster.

He held on to the memory of Liza turning to face him in the Monteleone suite. The last light of the day had streaked through her honeyed hair, and he'd thought he'd never seen anything more beautiful than she was at that moment. And he had walked away from her, promising he would return. Little had he suspected that she might be the one who would leave him.

"Tell me again about that note in the hotel room," Trent said.

The question drew Mike out of his depressing thoughts and he was glad for the diversion.

"It was meant to send you on a wild-goose chase— taking advantage of the fact that you already believed me to be the killer. Liza would have been safe with Joe, but you would have believed that I'd abducted her. It wasn't the best idea," Mike admitted, his worry for Liza making him regret that he'd ever approached her. Had he left her alone—had he remained in North Dakota—she would've been safe.

"If anything happens to her, it's my fault," Mike said. "I didn't kill Marcelle Ricco or Kyle LaRue, but if even a hair on Liza's head is harmed, I'll have to accept the burden of responsibility."

"Before we start assigning blame, let's see if we can't figure out what's going on and help her. Look." Trent gestured toward the side of the street where Familiar and Betta were hiding behind a trash can. "Isn't that her cat?"

"Familiar!" Mike leaped out of the car as the detective slowed it to a halt.

"They're inside," Betta said, nodding at the immaculately decorated duplex. "I saw Pascal come to the front door and look out. Then there was the sound of a trunk slamming. I think he has a car in that courtyard." She pointed.

As she spoke, the courtyard door began to slide back, revealing a big black Mercedes. Pascal was behind the wheel. When he saw Mike standing in the gutter, he gunned the engine and aimed the car directly at him.

"Yeow!" Familiar launched himself through the air, sailing through the open window of the car and landing on Pascal's head. The yowls mingled with screams of pain as Pascal fought the cat and attempted to drive the car.

"Betta!" Mike grabbed the psychic around the waist and dove with her to safety behind a pickup truck parked on the street. There was the sound of gunshots and suddenly the Mercedes swerved to a stop, both front tires shot cleanly out.

Trent walked to the driver's side, pulled the door open and jerked Pascal out of the disabled vehicle. "Where's Liza?" he demanded.

Mike knew. He scrambled to his feet and rushed to the trunk of the car. "Open it!" he demanded.

Pascal produced the key, tossing it to Mike.

When the trunk popped open, Mike thought his heart would break. Her body crumpled inside, Liza lay there, pale and unconscious. "Liza!" He picked her up in his arms, reassured by the warmth of her. When she moaned softly, he rocked her against his chest. "Call an ambulance," he said to Trent.

"No," Liza whispered, her eyes opening slowly. "I'm okay. I just have a splitting headache. It's Pascal. He murdered them both."

Mike carried Liza to the sidewalk where Betta had managed to obtain a glass of water. He held Liza gently in his arms as he watched Trent arrest Pascal, cuff him and send him away in a squad car.

The tall, blond detective then came toward him and Liza.

"I owe you an apology," he said. He shook his head as he looked at Liza. "And I owe you a lot more."

"You were only doing your job," Liza said softly. She sat up a little straighter and looked at Mike. "We both know you were only trying to do what's right, don't we?"

"You're a lucky man," Trent said. "A very lucky man. Liza never believed you were guilty."

"I know."

"Well, we'll have a few details to clear up, but as

far as the New Orleans Police Department is concerned, you're no longer a suspect. I wish you both the best of luck.''

Mike felt a grin spread over his face. "Thanks, Trent."

"Will you be going back to North Dakota?" Trent asked.

"Not immediately. I still have to regain my memory. And my future." He kissed Liza's cheek. "I've wasted a lot of years, and I don't want to let even a precious second slip away from us now."

*So, PASCAL IS BEHIND BARS and Liza and Duke are cozied up together on her sofa looking through old scrapbooks together. It seems that Duke is picking up on more and more of his past. He's even calling himself Duke now, instead of Mike. Such a relief for me! That Mike/Duke business was growing tiresome.*

*Tomorrow night, they're meeting Betta in Marcelle's house for a hypnosis session. Betta seems to think that the location will help Duke make a breakthrough with his past. What he doesn't remember, we've been able to piece together.*

*He was set up to go to Marcelle's. When he arrived, he found her body and was brutally beaten by Pascal and his band of thieves. They took his body to the train yard and dumped him in a boxcar, figuring he'd be found dead hundreds of miles away. But Duke was stronger than they expected, and he survived. Then his life in North Dakota began.*

*But now he's home, and Gabe and Rachel are on their way to The City that Care Forgot for the wedding of their adopted son. Liza and Duke are planning on living at the cattle ranch spring and fall and then com-*

ing to New Orleans for the summer. Liza can find new inspiration from the open vistas of the west, then refresh herself by painting the wonders of the city of her birth.

Things have a way of working out, and if Duke doesn't regain his memory, that's not the worst that can happen. So he doesn't have a past. Look at the people who don't have a future!

And I'm headed back to D.C. and my lovely Clotilde. Not to mention Eleanor, Dr. Dolittle and the marvelous little Jordan. And the new cake in the oven. I can't believe Eleanor is having another baby. I guess I'd better get some paying cases lined up if these youngsters are going to college.

Ah, what a beautiful spring evening. It does an old cat's heart good to watch lovers in love. Kiss her, Duke. She's waited more than five years for a moment like this.

I think I'll step out on the balcony and give them a bit of privacy. Wonder where my next mystery will take me? Well, no point in living in the past or the future. The present is good enough for this detective kitty.

# *Shh!*

## has a secret...

## *September 2000*

*You loved Gayle Wilson's original*
**MEN OF MYSTERY** *series so*
*much that we've brought it back!*

HARLEQUIN®

INTRIGUE®

*presents*

**Coming in August 2000**
**#578 RENEGADE HEART**
**Another exciting new story by**
**Gayle Wilson!**

Former CIA operative Drew Evans is a man on the
run. His only chance at life is Maggie Cannon, a
beautiful but vulnerable widow with a young
daughter to raise. But is she willing to help a
mysterious stranger…?

HARLEQUIN®
*Makes any time special* ™

If you enjoyed what you just read,
then we've got an offer you can't resist!

# Take 2 bestselling love stories FREE!

# Plus get a FREE surprise gift!

# HARLEQUIN®

# I N T R I G U E®

# COMING NEXT MONTH

Visit us at www.eHarlequin.com

CNM0600